THE PSYCHOLOGY OF BLACK LANGUAGE

About the Authors

JAMES HASKINS is Professor of English at the University of Florida, Gainesville, and lives in New York City. Author of more than 80 books for adult trade and young adult audiences, Haskins has won recognition for his work in both areas. Among his award-winning works are *The Story of Stevie Wonder*, *Count Your Way*, *Scott Joplin: The Man Who Made Ragtime* and *The Cotton Club*, which inspired the motion picture of the same name. Most recently, he co-authored a *Guide to the Black South* (Hippocrene 1993). Professor Haskins is currently on the National Education Advisory Committee of the Commission on the Bicentennial of the Constitution.

DR. HUGH F. BUTTS earned his M.D. at Meharry Medical College and completed his studies at the Columbia University Psychoanalytic Clinic for Training and Research. In addition to holding full professorships at Meharry Medical College and the Albert Einstein College of Medicine, he has held academic appointments at Columbia University, Atlanta University School of Social Work, Fordham University and the City College of New York. He is the author of one book, contributing author of three books, and has written over 100 scientific papers. He lives in New York with his wife Clementine and triplet daughters, Heather, Samantha, and Sydney.

THE PSYCHOLOGY OF BLACK LANGUAGE

James Haskins
Hugh F. Butts, M.D.

HIPPOCRENE BOOKS
New York

The authors are grateful for permission to reprint excerpts from the following books:

American Negro Folklore by J. Mason Brewer, Copyright © 1968 by J. Mason Brewer. Reprinted by permission of Quadrangle Books.
Die Nigger Die! by H. Rap Brown, Copyright © 1969 by Lynne Brown. Reprinted by permission of Dial Press and Allison and Busby.
Dutchman by LeRoi Jones, Copyright © 1964 by LeRoi Jones. Reprinted by permission of The Sterling Lord Agency, Inc.
Moby Dick by Herman Melville. Repinted by permission of The Macmillan Company.

For information, address:
HIPPOCRENE BOOKS, INC.
171 Madison Ave.
New York, NY 10016

ISBN 0-7818-0086-2

Printed in the United States of America.

Dedicated to Black people everywhere
because they and the rich and beautiful language they speak
are responsible for this book

Preface

It is very difficult to begin acknowledging here all the people, places, and things that are chiefly responsible for such an undertaking; but the authors wish to thank some important people here without whose help, inspiration, and dedication this book would have been impossible. Thanks to Ron Hobbs, to whose urging to do the research needed for such a work we finally succumbed. Thanks to Lorenzo D. Turner, whose many years of study and many fine books on black language made the research task easier. Thanks also to the many people who have done some initial work in the area of black languages and black dialects. Especially inspiring were LeRoi Jones's (Imamu Amiri Baraka's) *Blues People,* Lydia Parrish's *Slave Songs of the Georgia Sea Islands,* Edward L. Tinker's *Gombo Comes to Philadelphia,* Western Electric Company's audio presentation, "The Dialect of the Black American," and William A. Stewart's work at the Center for Applied Linguistics.

Thanks also to Barbara Schwartz, who typed the final draft and to Amy Shelansky, Pat Bruce, and Bella Rosenberg, who gave of their time and energy in research. And finally, to Kathy Benson, the one person most responsible for pulling the manuscript together into some literate, coherent form.

Hopefully, readers will not interpret the information presented here as final authority; new discoveries are being made in this area every day. Instead this should be viewed as an introductory work. The authors take all responsibility for it.

Contents

The Psychology of Black Language

"But 'glory' doesn't mean 'a nice knock-down argument,'" Alice objected.

"When I use a word," Humpty Dumpty said in rather a scornful tone, "it means just what I choose it to mean—neither more nor less."

"The question is," said Alice, "whether you can make words mean so many different things."

"The question is," said Humpty Dumpty, "which is to be Master—that's all."

Lewis Carroll, *Through the Looking Glass*

Introduction

The authors feel that this work represents a unique contribution to the ever-increasing body of literature dealing with the black experience. The collaborators are a black educator and a black psychoanalyst, who from their respective vantage points and frames of reference have examined the development and uses of verbal behavior (language) among blacks. Verbal behavior is one of the areas of the black experience that has been accorded scant exploration, and thus it was with this recognition, combined with an interest in the area and a desire to make a new contribution, that the authors embarked upon the writing of this book. As with many such ventures, areas for further investigation developed as the authors synthesized their thoughts on the subject of language in blacks. At certain junctures we had to admit that we did not have a definitive answer, but that at least new hypotheses had arisen.

Crucial to any understanding of current verbal behavior in blacks are several parameters that the authors examine:

1. The psychology of oppression, and the role of verbal behavior as a tool for dealing with oppression.
2. The African origins of current black verbal behavior and manifestations of those roots in current black language.
3. The development of verbal behavior among blacks during infancy and childhood.
4. The evolution of various dialects among blacks.

Although the subject is language, there are obvious applications to other dimensions of the black experience: for example, psychology, sociology, anthropology, history, and politics. In fact, language

1

is so basic to all of the aforementioned disciplines that no investigation of the black experience in any one of them can aspire to comprehensiveness without considering the role of language.

The authors were heartened as well as disappointed as they took stock of the literature and discovered that there was no book that dealt with the topic so extensively as this one: heartened because of the singularity of the task, disappointed because such a vital area had been neglected. We feel that this is a definitive work, which should serve as a catalyst for further study and writing.

1
The Development
of Language

Language, or verbal behavior, is an adaptive technique unique to human beings. The acquisition of language skills is an extremely complicated feat, one whose difficulty is compounded by the other developmental tasks simultaneously confronting the infant. In learning language, the baby is not only learning to communicate verbally, but he is also assimilating the culture's system of meanings and its ways of thinking and reasoning.[1] Each society categorizes experience somewhat differently, and the vocabulary of its language forms a catalogue of the categories it uses in perceiving, thinking, and communicating.[2] The importance of the mother, or mothering person, as mediator between the developing infant and the outer world is obvious. This role is also crucial in the development of verbal behavior. Piaget emphasizes the imitative aspect of the acquisition of language. He feels that language is acquired by the child through meaningful imitation, just as are motoric gestures. He underscores "meaningful" to stress again the fact that imitation, though it may at times appear to be a copy of an external model, is never merely a passive copy; imitation is always linked to an active scheme of knowing, even though the knowing may not be very profound.[3]

When one considers the development of verbal behavior in black infants, the maternal role of mediator is seen as crucial also to the outer society's impact upon the infant. The methodological frame of reference of this book is adaptational in that it examines ways in which verbal behavior in blacks may be adaptive or maladaptive, depending on whether or not need gratification occurs. A social system's approach to black family interaction posits the developing infant at the center of a circle of layers: first, the black family; next, the black community; and finally the wider society. The black family is imbedded in a network of mutually interdependent relationships with the Negro community and the wider society. The Negro community includes within itself a number of institutions which may also be viewed as subsystems. Prominent among these are schools, churches, taverns, newspapers, neighborhood associations, lodges, and so on. The wider society consists of major institutions which help set the conditions for black life. Chief among these are the subsystem of values, the political, economic, education, health, welfare, and communication subsystems.[4] A previous statement must be underscored in the context of this social systems model: *In learning language, the baby is not only learning to communicate verbally, but he is also assimilating the culture's system of meanings and its ways of thinking and reasoning.*

EARLY LANGUAGE DEVELOPMENT

How does the infant learn verbal behavior? The foundations upon which the acquisition of language is built are laid down in the first year, along with the mutual understanding between child and parents of needs, wishes, feelings, and intentions. The capacity to develop speech is an innate human attribute and all infants start to babble. The infant's babbling is reinforced not only by his hearing of it, but by the vocalizations of others which encourage him to experiment vocally. Lewis believes that there are archetypal nursery words that are ubiquitous. These are repetitions of the vowel "ah" with different consonants (for example, "nana," "baba," "papa").[5] Certain repetitive sounds are selected and repeated by parents. The baby's speech starts with the archetypal sounds that are reinforced by his parents. His parents cause these archetypal sounds to denote something. In a sense parents speak baby language and then with the passage of time use words that approximate the real word.

As the infant adds a new word to his increasing vocabulary, the new word initially has an expanded meaning, which is gradually narrowed to appropriate usage. Piaget found that soon after his thirteen-month-old daughter learned "bow-wow," she pointed to a dog while standing on her balcony and said "bow-wow," and thereafter the word was used for anything seen from her balcony, including horses, baby carriages, cars, and people; and not until three months later was "bow-wow" reserved for dogs. The process of expansion and contraction of word usage is extremely complicated. Again, as with the initial vocalizations of the infant, the contraction of sounds is under the aegis and responsive guidance of those who share in the infant's experiences. The word gradually gains a discrete meaning and becomes a symbol as it comes to designate the unity and identity of the subject as perceived from different perspectives and in different situations; and also when different objects with the same critical attributes are categorized together by the same word.[6]

FAMILY MODELS

From all that has been said so far, it is apparent that the child's language development depends largely upon those parental figures or other meaningful people in the immediate milieu who can understand the child's nonverbal communication and, by continually interacting with him, facilitate his linguistic maturation. It is fascinating at this point to speculate in an area which to the authors' knowledge has not been addressed. Piaget and others have emphasized the mother's vital role in the development of verbal behavior in children. It seems reasonable to assume that her presence in the household during the phase of language development would facilitate that development. Traditional development models have emphasized the maternal role in key areas of the infant's development. Few models have suggested that additional mothering or nurturing figures could influence infantile development positively. The model of the nuclear family as the optimum one for child-rearing completely discounts other forms of family life that have proven extremely adaptive among blacks.

Billingsley describes the *simple nuclear family* as one consisting of husband and wife with their own or adopted children living together in their own household with no other members present. This is the traditional type of family structure in America and Europe. Among students of the family, it is considered the ideal but not universal family form.[7] In the *extended family,* other relatives are introduced into the nuclear household. *Augmented families* are those in which unrelated individuals, such as boarders, live. In 1965 there were "nearly a half million Negro persons living with family groups with whom they were not related by marriage, ancestry, or adoption. . . . In 1965, nearly 15 percent of all Negro families had one or more minor relations living with them who was not their own child."[8] Billingsley differentiates between the expressive and the instrumental functions of the family. Both functions are highly interrelated, especially in the areas of sex, reproduction, and child-rearing. The authors' hypothesis is that the expressive instrumental axis of family functioning, particularly in the area of child-rearing (including the development of verbal behavior), is facilitated by the evolution of extended and augmented families, because other meaningful figures also provide reinforcement, feedback, and linguistic models for developing infants. The nuclear family bias has resulted in a dismal failure to examine the adaptive features of other forms of family life (extended and augmented families among blacks).

SOME THEORIES OF LANGUAGE

Julius Lester regards Western culture as one which seeks to separate object and subject by the introduction of verbs, adjectives, and so on.[9] Black verbal expression, on the other hand, tends to be much more direct, with no interposition between subject and object. It is such directness that characterizes the black experience.

In the chapter "The Negro and Language" in *Black Skin, White Masks,* Frantz Fanon, beginning with his belief that "to speak is to exist absolutely for the other,"[10] describes ways in which language and its uses serve to reinforce the subjugated position of the black colonial. Fanon's thesis is that language affords power. The subjugation of colonized peoples is facilitated by the "death and burial of its local cultural originality." To the extent that the subjugated colonial can adopt the mother country's cultural standards, he becomes whiter and renounces his blackness. The white colonial tends to stereotype the native and deny him access to the mother culture by speaking nigger-pidgin to him.

The interface between language and psychology is not only an extremely involved area, but still is in an infant investigative state. One notable theoretician, George A. Miller,[11] offers as a "map" of language and psychology a logico-philosophical frame of reference in which the study of signs and symbols is divided into three parts: syntactics, semantics, and pragmatics. Syntactic studies are concerned with the relation of signs to signs. Semantics deals with the relation of signs to their meanings. Pragmatics is concerned with the relation of signs to the people who use them. This scheme "is a way of thinking about the psychological process involved in linguistic knowledge and behavior . . . it leads you into a kind of hierarchy of process: At the lowest level it is necessary to understand the syntactic structure; then it becomes possible to understand its semantic content; and at the top, after both structural analysis and semantic comprehension are achieved, pragmatic acceptance or rejection is possible."[12]

There is controversy in the area of psycholinguistics as to whether emphasis should be placed on theories of language or theories of language users. However, fortunately, these areas overlap so that the linguist tests his formulation of the rules of the language and the psychologist tests his formulation of the psychological processes whereby the language user succeeds or fails in obeying these rules. Accordingly, an extremely profitable arena for investigation is the pragmatic study of language (construction of theories of language users).

Productivity is a characteristic of language. Linguistic rules are referred to as habits, and these habits are those that human beings are uniquely prepared to acquire. There is, so to speak, a large nativistic component in our ability and proclivity for acquiring linguistic rules.[13] Miller cites a variety of psycholinguistic phenomena that may serve as useful examples of the establishment of habit and productivity in language. For our purposes, reference to the use of "negative instances" is quite germane. Smoke stated explicitly that "negative instances" of any given concept are more difficult for people to understand and use than are positive instances.[14] Hovlandus and Weiss demonstrated the superiority of position instances when the informational value of both positive and negative instances had been carefully controlled in advance.[15] Wason showed that it takes longer to evaluate negative sentences than positive ones.[16] This type of investigation, while very exciting, throws open for speculation black linguistic adaptations, which in many instances have resulted in negative sentences being used for greater emphasis than positive sentences.

LANGUAGE AND INTELLIGENCE

The study of language and language development has obvious and relevant implications for the study of cognitive functioning.

Controversy has continued ad nauseam about intelligence in blacks as opposed to intelligence in whites. A crude definition of intelligence is "the ability to operate effectively with symbols."[17] A meaningful definition of intelligence should also include a capacity for learning in general, for learning at the level of principles, and for symbolic elaboration. It is likewise clear that effective intelligence requires various personal qualities: sensibility, sympathy, balance, flexibility, humor, detachment, drive, and the capacity for self-criticism.[18] Another important consideration in evaluating intelligence is "tolerance of ambiguity,"[19] or resistance to premature closure, to jumping to conclusions. Intelligence is usually assessed in tests of factual knowledge, reasoning, memory, word knowledge, arithmetic, spatial visualization, and knowledge of social conventions. Some intelligence tests call for verbal responses, whereas others require the manipulation of concrete materials.

If we assume that a group of people have had equal opportunities for intellectual development, then those who have profited the most from their opportunities should be the most intelligent. Critics have pointed out, however, that the assumption of equality of opportunity is a very dubious one. The black child growing up in Mississippi has an opportunity to learn a great many things, but these things differ from those to which a white child in Boston is exposed and which he grows up with and assimilates. If middle class children excel in the kind of intelligence that shows up on intelligence tests and in school learning, there is little doubt that the lower class black child excels in practical intelligence as measured by ability to fend for oneself. (This has been termed "street knowledge.")

Intelligence tests do two things: first, they test for passive knowledge, and, second, they test for the ability to perform various kinds of cognitive operations—to think. These tests are based on verbal behavior which develops along different lines in poor black children than in white children. Consequently, one may question the reliability of these tests as true measures of intelligence in black children. The area of cognition is even more complicated. Hess and Shipman, in describing cultural deprivation, conclude: "The meaning of deprivation is a deprivation of meaning—a cognitive environment in which behavior is controlled by status roles rather than by attention to the individual characteristics of a specific situation and one in which behavior is not mediated by verbal cues or by teaching that relates events to one another and the present to the future. This environment produces a child who relates to authority rather than to rationale; who, although often compliant, is not reflective in his behavior, and for whom the consequences of an act are largely considered in terms of immediate punishment or reward rather than future effects and long-range goals."[20] The emphasis of these investigators is almost exclusively on child-mother interaction as the mediator of cognitive modes.

LANGUAGE AND SELF-DEVELOPMENT

Until now we have dealt with the early development of language, the role of nurturing figures in the development of verbal behavior, cognitive skills, and intelligence. Language is obviously also related to the development of the self. In this theory's most simplistic formulation, the self is based in part on others' attitudes toward the developing organism, and in part on the developing organism's attitude toward itself. This dual origin may represent conflict. "They see me as ——— + I see me as ——— = Self." Stated somewhat differently,[21] there are two general stages in the full development of the self. At the first of these stages, the individual's self is constituted simply by an organization of the particular attitudes of this individual toward himself and toward others in the specific social acts in which he participates with them. But at the second stage in the full development of the individual's self, that self is constituted not only by an organization of these particular attitudes but also by an organization of the social attitudes of the generalized other or the social group as a whole to which he belongs. Language in its significant sense is that vocal gesture which tends to arouse in the individual the attitude which it arouses in others, and it is this perfecting of the self by the gesture which mediates the social activities that gives rise to the process of taking the role of the other.[22]

THE DEVELOPMENT OF VERBAL BEHAVIOR IN BLACKS

There has as yet been little research in the area of the development of verbal behavior in black children and adults. The assumption that this development proceeds along the same lines as it does in white children and adults is unfounded, since a variety of factors indigenous to the black experience might affect language development. Many cogent and thus far unanswered questions arise from the differential development between blacks and whites, for example:

1. How does black family organization effect the acquisition of cognition skills?

2. How does the relationship between the developing individual and his milieu affect his verbal behavior?

3. What kinds of cognitive skills need to be acquired by the pre-school child to assure him of academic success?

4. How may the mass communication media (e.g., the *Sesame Street* television program) facilitate the development of cognitive behavior and verbal behavior in black ghetto children?

The interrelationships between self-esteem, cognitive behavior, verbal behavior, and the mass media have been pointed up by the *Sesame Street* program. Joan Cooney, testifying before the Senate Select Committee on Equal Educational Opportunity (Washington, D.C., July 30, 1971), said: "We were advised that the Black inner city child has a lower opinion of his intellectual capacity than his white middle class counterpart. Our approach to this problem was to design a program that would present the child with an abundance of success experiences. . . . Numerous observations we have made indicate that during the course of the program the children became more and more confident of their own ability and began to regard themselves as learners."[23] This program series also influenced parental expectations with respect to learning, teacher attitudes, and racial attitudes. Many children in our society grow up in segregated communities. Black children do not have much opportunity to know whites intimately, nor do white children have the opportunity to know blacks. When they are confronted with people who look so different from themselves, this unfamiliarity may lead to fear which triggers negative attitudes toward those who are different.

The development of verbal behavior is extremely complicated in black children because of unique aspects of the black experience (e.g., family organization; interaction among families, the black community, and the wider society; the impact of the mass media upon cognitive development in black children; and the effect of institutionalized racism on language development and learning ability).

RELATION OF LANGUAGE TO OTHER FORMS OF BEHAVIOR

In Chapter 2, "The Psychology of Oppression," the authors examine the varieties of adaptations and maladaptations of blacks to oppressive, racist institutions. The inclusion of a chapter on oppression in a book on black language is pertinent because language is behavior, and, like other forms of behavior, it is affected by intrapsychic factors as well as by institutional arrangements and practices. It behooves us, therefore, to continue our investigation of language in blacks by establishing a correlation between language (verbal behavior) and other forms of behavior. Some of the examples cited will be quite obvious, others more subtle.

Obsessive-compulsive behavior refers to behavioral characteristics such as rigidity, punctuality, parsimoniousness, isolation of affects, and repression or retroflexion of rage. The individual who utilizes these behavioral manifestations is referred to as an obsessional character. In contradistinction, hysterical behavior as exemplified by the hysterical personality is characterized by flamboyance; freedom of affectivity; disdain for punctuality, rigidity, and schedules; and by a histrionic flair. Verbal behavior in the two groups (obsessional character and hysterical character) also tends to be distinctive and at times diagnostic. The verbal behavior of the obsessive-compulsive is precise, intellectualized, and lacking in spontaneity and affect. The verbal behavior of the hysteric is overflowing in affective terms, florid, and lacking in precision and accuracy. These two examples are excellent points of departure because each represents the antithesis of the other. To cite a somewhat exaggerated example, in response to the question, "What's the weather like today?" an obsessive-compulsive might reply, "It's warm, but not as warm as yesterday; the sky is somewhat, but not overly hazy and it may rain, although I doubt it. On the other hand it may not rain." The hysteric might simply reply, "Gray day—makes me feel blah and gloomy." Similar correlations could be elaborated for the paranoid, passive-aggressive, and passive-dependent personalities.

How does this discourse relate to language in blacks? Obviously a black obsessive-compulsive will tend to use obsessional verbal behavior; a black hysteric will tend to use hysterical verbal behavior, and so on. These are fairly clear-cut distinctions rooted in personality formation, defensive formation, conflict, and symptom formation. One cannot ascribe the verbal behavior of the obsessional black to institutionalized racism, just as one cannot ascribe acute paranoid schizophrenia in a black to institutionalized racism. In all honesty, all that can be hypothesized is that, because of its ubiquity, racism may have contributed to the condition. How then can oppression be related to the verbal behavior of any particular black?

In LeRoi Jones's play *Dutchman,* Clay, a young black man en route to a party, is approached on the subway by Lula, a white woman. She engages him in conversation and soon begins to chip away at his composure and reserved facade until he retaliates in kind.

Lula touches on Clay's pseudo-obsessionalism with her comment: "You look like you live in New Jersey with your parents and are trying to grow a beard. That's what you look like you've been reading Chinese poetry and drinking warm sugarless tea. You look like death eating a soda cracker." Her goal is not solely the oppression of Clay but his destruction (which she eventually achieves). Her tactic is the extremely clever one of stripping away his obsessional defenses so that with his raw rage exposed she can feel justified in murdering him. He "socks it to her": "You great liberated whore! You fuck some black man, and right away you're an expert on black people. What a lotta shit that is. The only thing you know is that you come if he bangs you hard enough, and that's all. The belly rub? You wanted to do the belly rub? Shit, you don't even know how. You don't know how. That ol' dipty-dip shit you do, rolling your ass like an elephant, that's not my kind of belly rub. Belly rub is not Queens. Belly rub is dark places, with big hats and overcoats held up with one arm. Belly rub hates you."[24]

Clay is talking like a black nigger who has dropped his obsessional facade and is responding to twenty-one years of racism—is "letting it all hang out." But rage is not the all-important ingredient of his statement. What frightens, infuriates, and humiliates Lula is the accuracy, sensitivity, truth, perceptiveness, and "black directness" of his accusations. She strips him and herself winds up denuded except for her stiletto, which she uses to silence his truth forever.

Oppression, racism, and discrimination have posited a two-horned dilemma for blacks: repress rage and be verbally obsessive or let it all hang out and be *expressive* (not only of rage but also of love). Lula is confronted with her incapacity for love by a man who knows what love is and can express it. His dying comment is "Sorry, baby, I don't think we could make it."

EFFECTS OF OPPRESSION ON BLACK VERBAL BEHAVIOR

The interface between oppression and verbal behavior is even more complicated. One may consider verbal behavior in blacks as serving several functions: (1) as a defense against individualized ✓ and institutionalized racist behavior in whites; (2) as an aspect of the black life style reflecting healthy group narcissism, cohesive bonds, and affection; (3) as an avenue for the release of rage, fear, guilt, and other affects on an individual basis.

In many respects, the development of verbal behavior in black Americans parallels the development of their music (another form of oral expression). Throughout the years blacks have evolved forms of expression which are unique, spontaneous, and extremely communicative. Ben Sidran in *Black Talk* comments: "Recently, this ability of the oral culture to generate its own style of spontaneous leadership, rather than depend on imposed, more formalized leadership, was reported by Stokeley Carmichael as his major reason for having left America. 'I know I cannot provide the leadership right now in America. . . . that's the beauty of black people—spontaneity will be our saving . . . because that means the CIA cannot pinpoint our leadership and destroy the movement.' "[25] This is reminiscent of the ghetto humor that surfaced during the Watts movement: "Chuck (the white man) don't know where it's gonna happen next cause we don't know ourselves."[26]

In Sidran's opinion, the black oral culture is primarily a living, organic organization, rather than a technocratic structure, and as such it rails against comfort mentalization. Black verbal expression thrives on what should appear to the analytic mind as emotional paradoxes. As an example, the lyrics of one song are "I can't stand you baby, but I need you—you're bad, but you're oh so good," and of another song, "I have the blues, they hurt so nice."

This ability to deal with seemingly contradictory affects is characteristic of black verbal behavior. The psychological implications are vast. Erik Erikson, in *Childhood and Society,* refers to white psycho-social character formation in terms of certain polarities in thinking that affect childhood development.[27] Some of these polarities are migratory versus sedentary, individualistic versus standardized, competitive versus cooperative, and pious versus free thinking. Difficulty in integrating such polarities necessitates or brings about the retention of one aspect of the polarity, and the projection of the other aspect. This is in part a learned response which is constantly reinforced by parental behavior: "Mom is the unquestioned authority in matters of mores and morals in her home, yet she permits herself to remain vain in her appearance, egotistical in her demands, and infantile in her emotions. In any situation in which this discrepancy clashes with the respect she demands from her children, she blames her children, she never blames herself. She thus maintains the discontinuity between the child's and the adult's status."[28]

CONCLUSION

As previously noted, something in the black experience permits the simultaneous existence of contradictions. This quality of black verbal behavior may be a source of consternation to whites but is accepted by blacks as "the way it's spose to be." Verbal behavior in blacks may be viewed solely as a response or adaptation to oppression. This would be too restrictive a view and would lose sight of those aspects of the black experience that are healthy manifestations of group love and cohesion and of the development of affectionate bonds between blacks. It is our contention that a great deal of verbal behavior among blacks serves the purpose of expressing a variety of thoughts and feelings *not* in answer to racism or repression. This viewpoint considers blacks not as mere passive respondents to an alien and hostile society but as people who have brought, originated, and transmitted certain unique mores and values to create a culture that has survived continual efforts to annihilate it.

2
The Psychology
of Oppression

The key to an understanding of ways in which language has developed and been utilized by black Americans is the concept of the psychological impact of oppression. In order to appreciate the variety of techniques developed by blacks to cope with oppression, it is necessary first to define adaptation.

Adaptation refers to the psychological devices the human being employs in his social environment in order to ensure his health and his survival. Good health depends upon the satisfaction of needs. Physiological needs are inborn, functional expressions of the structural organization of the body. Unlike physiological needs, social needs are not innate. They develop only after exposure to the society into which an individual has been born, and their nature is determined by the demands of that society. The filling of such needs as those for status, prestige, and conformity to convention not only relieves anxiety about social exclusion but also rewards performance considered socially useful. The adaptations required to satisfy these needs will vary with the cultural institutions of a society. Behavioral patterns are adaptive if they result in the human organism's attainment of health and survival. Behavioral patterns are maladaptive if they do not secure health and survival. Adaptation and maladaptation are extremely useful concepts when one considers the institutions to which black Americans must adapt.

ROOTS OF WHITE RACISM

Pinderhughes's definition of racism as *"pro-white, anti-black paranoia"*[1] carries with it a number of implications. First, paranoia indicates the projection onto black people of unacceptable impulses

15

and views held by white people. This tendency is enforced by the lowly position, constant denigration, disenfranchisement, and mistreatment accorded blacks ("They must be inferior if they are treated in that way"). The "pro-white, anti-black" aspect may be initiated by perceptions of bodily organization that underscores the cephalo-caudal mode of development, so that cephalad body parts are viewed with dignity, while hind portions are viewed with disdain. The tendency to dichotomize the body and its concrete external representations may be one aspect of human development that relates to subjugation of the "inferior" types.

The impact of oppression upon the lowly oppressed requires no further elaboration. The toll on the master, however, has been accorded minimal attention. Whenever one human being predicates his sense of dignity and self-esteem on the subjugation of another human being, he is sick, although he may be living according to the dictates of a racist system. "If a group is different in appearance, culture, and behavior—particularly when a low or shamefully denigrated value is given the specific differences—the group can be associated with low things . . . the bottom, buttocks, genitals, and sexuality."[2]

In the words of Kardiner and Ovesey, "Slavery was the extreme manifestation of the age's perversion of dominance—the subjection of another human being to a pure utilitarian use."[3] Once you degrade someone in that way, the sense of guilt makes it imperative to degrade the object further in order to justify the entire procedure. If you do not use the human being whose attributes you despise, you can escape the ambit of his influence by sheer avoidance; if you use him, you cannot avoid the consequences. The only defense now is to *hate* the object. However, when the enslaved person is compliant and servile, this hatred can remain hidden and its place taken by condescension. Should the enslaved become refractory, then the hatred can emerge clearly; but when it does, the reasons seem very different from what they were when the slave was compliant. Now the reason for the hatred becomes the loss of dominance over an object that has already been degraded in status. This represents a claim by the Negro for a reciprocal emotional relation with the white, and hence a fall in status for the white.

EFFECTS OF SLAVERY

The types of adaptation to slave status utilized by blacks consisted of (1) overt aggression, revolt, or flight; (2) passivity or submissiveness and the plea for rescue; (3) the vicarious aggression in the folk tales (see Uncle Remus); (4) suicide (most instances of which occurred shortly after capture).

When the countries of Europe undertook to develop the New World, they were interested primarily in the exploitation of America's natural resources. Labor was necessary, and at first the most promising source seemed to be Indians. Indian labor, however, proved unsatisfactory for various reasons, and the search for acceptable labor in large quantities led to the slave trade in Africa.

The character of slavery and the plantation system in the United States was in marked contrast to that in other parts of the New World. In the West Indies and Brazil, large numbers of African slaves were concentrated on vast plantations for the production of sugar. Under such conditions it was possible for the slaves to reestablish their African ways of life and to keep their traditions alive. But in the United States, the slaves were scattered on plantations and farms in relatively small numbers over a large area. In 1860, in the South as a whole, three-fourths of the farms and plantations had fewer than fifty slaves. The inhuman practice of separating families contributed further to the vitiation of African culture among the slaves. The twenty Africans brought to Virginia in 1619 were indentured servants, but by the year 1670, the slave status of Negroes imported into Virginia was fixed by law.

There is variance among historians and sociologists as to the extent to which African culture survived the transmutation to a new environment. Herskovits[4] believes that African survivals can be discovered in almost every phase of current Negro life; Frazier disagrees.[5] However, the question of cultural survival versus cultural extinction is not so germane as the issue of the social adaptation of the blacks to the American culture. Slavery demolished the traces of African culture sufficiently to necessitate an adaptation to predominant American cultural mores. The adaptive process among blacks carried with it several implications: (1) old types of organization were rendered useless; (2) the minimal conditions for maintaining a culture or for developing a new one were lacking; and (3) the adoption of American culture was limited. The adaptive process was rendered difficult, complicated, and at times impossible by the master race's definition of the slaves' inferior status.

Not only was the African culture of the slaves destroyed but reciprocal interaction between master and slave was impeded and free emotional interaction between slaves was impaired. Marriage among slaves often was not recognized; paternity was not recognized. Offspring became the property of whoever owned the mother; the child-mother relationship had to be respected at least until the utility potential of the child was realized. The Negro woman did have the opportunity for more emotional interaction with white masters by virtue of her sexual attractiveness. The white child's attachment to the black mammy often predisposed the white man to view the Negro woman as a sexual object. The need for laws prohibiting marriage between whites and blacks was an eloquent testimonial to the black woman's attractiveness to the white man (and vice versa).

Kardiner and Ovesey[6] regard the salient features of slaves' status adaptation as (1) degradation of self-esteem; (2) destruction of cultural forms and forced adoption of foreign culture traits; (3) destruction of the family unit, with particular disparagement to the male; (4) relative enhancement of the female status, thus making her the central figure in the culture; (5) the destruction of social cohesion among Negroes by the inability to have their own culture; (6) the idealization of the white master—but with this ideal was incorporated an object that was at once revered and hated.

EFFECTS OF STEREOTYPES

In what ways did slavery influence subsequent institutional formation in America? The definitions of blacks as violent, inferior, promiscuous, and irresponsible have given rise to certain institutional practices that serve to perpetuate these definitions. Thus, the definition of black people as violent encourages police actions that provoke violent group reactions among black people. Repressive and insulting social attitudes that incite violent reactions in individual blacks are encouraged. Policemen are the purveyors of the values of the society in which they live. In early September, 1968, approximately 150 off-duty policemen, members of an organization known as the "Law Enforcement Society," attacked a group of Black Panthers in New York City's Criminal Court Building. Police Commissioner Howard R. Leary in commenting on the attack said, "They [white policemen] are reflecting the community. They are responsive to what they believe the community wants."[7]

The adaptations and maladaptations that black people have made in response to their characterization as violent include (1) excessive repression and suppression of normal hostile responses with somatization and with compensatory techniques for emotional catharsis; (2) identification with the aggressor and the development of complementary conscience defects; (3) "acting out" of socially assigned roles; (4) emphasis on emotional as opposed to intellectual values, because of a distrust of intellectually expressed values of American society; (5) self-derogation; (6) the utilization of a variety of defense mechanisms.

SKIN-COLOR PERCEPTION AND SELF-ESTEEM

A study by one of the authors was designed to demonstrate the interrelationship between blacks' perception of their skin color and their corresponding level of self-esteem.[8] One of the psychological consequences of racial oppression is a lowering of self-esteem resulting from an identification with the aggressor and an incorporation of his values.

There were two variables in this study: self-esteem (the independent variable) and perception of skin color (the dependent variable). There was no need for a control group since we were primarily interested in the concomitance of variation between the independent and dependent variable.

Self-esteem was measured by testing the subjects with the California Test of Personality (C.T.P.), Elementary Series, 1953 Revision. One of the subtests is entitled "Sense of Personal Worth." The reliability coefficient of this subtest is .79 and the standard error 1.49 (standardized with 648 cases). This test is regarded as one of the better personality inventory tests available. In addition to the California Test of Personality, a rating scale was utilized as a measure of self-esteem. The subjects were rated by their social workers and counselors. The self-esteem rating scale was dichotomized as follows: 1, 2, 3—poor; 4, 5—good.

The Test. A test devised by Kenneth Clark and Mamie Clark was utilized to measure the dependent variable, perception of skin color. The experimental group consisted of fifty children: twenty-four boys and twenty-six girls. All subjects were in the age range 9–12, had I.Q.s above 80, and had no clinical or Rorschach evidence of integrative pathology. The test consisted of a sheet of paper on which were the outline drawings of a leaf, apple, mouse, and boy (when the test was administered to boys) or girl (in the case of girls). Each child was provided with a 64-crayon Crayola set, including white, black, and the following shades of brown: raw umber, sepia, raw sienna, brown, burnt sienna, tan, and "flesh." Each child was asked first to color the objects and the mouse in order to determine whether there was a stable concept of the relationship of color to object. If the child passed this portion (see Table 1) he was then told, "Color this little boy (or girl) the color

Table 1

CALIFORNIA TEST OF PERSONALITY PERSONAL WORTH SCALE: EXPERIMENTAL DATA

	Number Tested	Score Median	Number Pass	Percent Pass	Number Fail	Percent Fail
Boys	24	8	17	34	7	14
Girls	26	7	20	40	6	12
Total	50	7	37	74	13	26

that you are." He was then told, "Now this is a little girl (or boy). Color her (or him) the color you like little boys (or girls) to be. Responses were classified as either reality responses, phantasy responses, or escape responses. A reality response was regarded as one which was within three shadings of the subject's skin color. The subject's skin color was rated by having the tester compare the subject's skin color to the most appropriate crayon of the set. A phantasy response was rated as one more than three shadings from the subject's skin color. An escape response was regarded as a bizarre one (e.g., red or blue). Verbal responses and behavior of the subjects during the test were recorded. The author administered the color test, and it was scored by an independent judge, that is, by a person who was not acquainted with the children.

Results. The experimental results are presented in tabular form in Tables 1 and 2. All the scales have been dichotomized: the self-esteem ratings in terms of good and poor; color test responses in terms of pass and fail; and the C.T.P. in terms of pass or fail with the group median (7) as the dividing point. With this dichotomization it became a simple matter to apply phi coefficient to test the correlation between the two traits, self-esteem and color perception.

Table 2

COLOR TEST: FIGURE 1

Children Tested	Number Pass	Percent Pass	Number Fail	Percent Fail	Number Phantasy	Percent Phantasy	Number Escape	Percent Escape
Boys	17	34	7	14	6	12	1	2
Girls	19	38	7	14	6	12	1	2
Total	36	72	14	28	12	24	2	4

COLOR TEST: FIGURE 2

Children Tested	Number Reality	Percent Reality	Number Phantasy	Percent Phantasy	Number Escape	Percent Escape
Boys	11	22	10	20	3	6
Girls	13	26	12	24	1	2
Total	24	48	22	44	4	8

Table 3

CORRELATIONAL DATA

Correlations	ø	X^2
C.T.P. and color test	.44	9.68
Social worker's self-esteem ratings and color test	.196	1.80
Counselor's self-esteem ratings and color test	.08	.30

Since there is no way of finding confidence limits for ø (phi coefficient), it became necessary to establish chi square by using the formula: chi square $(X^2) - Nø^2$, where N equals the number of subjects; and then, by referring $Nø^2$ to a chi square, limits were established for three conditions:

1. C.T.P. sense of personal worth and color test.
2. Social worker's ratings of self-esteem and the color test.
3. Counselor's ratings of self-esteem and the color test.

These results are shown in Table 4. The only correlation which confirmed the hypothesis was the first: between the California Test of Personality and the color test. One would have expected a more significant correlation between the social worker's and counselor's ratings and the color test.

Table 4
RESULTS OF CORRELATIONS

Correlations	∅	X^2
Correlations between Figures 1 and 2	.54	.15
Correlation between Figure 2 and social worker's rating	.20	2.0
Correlation between Figure 2 and counselor's rating	.09	.4
Correlation between Figure 2 and C.T.P.	.20	2.0

The hypothesis is confirmed by the concomitance between the test for self-esteem and ratings of color tests.

Summary. In summary fifty Negro children between the ages of nine and twelve were given the California Test of Personality in order to rate their self-esteem. This group was also rated as to their self-esteem by social workers and counselors on a 1 to 5 scale. The children were given a coloring test in which they were asked to color two figures: the first their color, the second the color they like children to be. Fourteen of the fifty children misperceived their own color, and of this number eight failed the test of self-esteem, for a phi coefficient of .44 and a chi-square value of 9.68 (significant at the 1 percent level of confidence). Counselors' and social workers' ratings did not correlate significantly with the color test results. Thirteen of the fourteen subjects who failed to perceive themselves accurately on the first figure, showed a preference for children who were lighter or white on the second figure. The hypothesis that a group of Negro children with impaired self-esteem would perceive themselves less accurately in terms of skin color was borne out.

It would be fascinating to duplicate this study with a similar population in the 1970s. The authors' hypothesis is that black consciousness, the emphasis on "Black is beautiful," would produce different results at this time than eight years ago. Many more children would probably tend to identify positively with blackness and would show a corresponding increase in their self-esteem levels.

CONTRIBUTION OF FANON

Frantz Fanon contributed extensively to our current understanding of the nature and psychological effects of oppression. While a psychiatrist by training, he was a Marxist politically, and he never lost sight of the economic base of racism and colonialism. In his first book, *Black Skin, White Masks,* published in 1952, his avowed purpose was to analyze and dissipate the racist relationship between blacks and whites: "I believe that the fact of the juxtaposition of the white and black races has created a massive psychoexistential complex. I hope by analyzing to destroy it."[9]

"The analysis that I am undertaking," Fanon stated, "is psychological. In spite of this it is apparent to me that the effective disalienation of the Black man entails an immediate recognition of social and economic realities. If there is an inferiority complex, it is the outcome of a double process primarily economic, subsequently, the internalization or, better, the epidermalization of this inferiority."[10]

In the chapter entitled "The Fact of Blackness" (*Peau Noir*), Fanon described the effects of white racist practices on his own self-esteem: "It was always the Negro teacher, the Negro doctor, brittle as I was becoming, I shivered at the slightest pretext. I knew, for instance, that if the physician made a mistake it would be the end of him and of all those who came after him. . . . The black physician can never be sure how close he is to disgrace. I tell you, I was walled in: No exception was made for my refined manners, or my knowledge of literature, or my understanding of the quantum theory."[11]

Fanon's primary message in *Black Skin, White Masks* is a description of the variety of techniques by which the black native is coerced into living his "inbred racial guilt." In the Antilles as in France, school children were reared on stories in which the black man symbolized the forces of evil. It was all very well to go to the movies in Fort-de-France to laugh at the wild antics of Bushmen and Zulus, and to support Tarzan against the malevolent blacks, but to sit in a French cinema in the face of the same rubbish was a petrifying experience. In the context of a white audience, the Negro, whether he liked it or not, found himself identified with the Bushmen and Zulus. He was condemned.[12] Thus the Negro Antillian aspired to be white.

The unconscious racist techniques utilized to enslave and denigrate the black in the Antilles do not differ significantly from those same techniques used in any oppressive society. These techniques are ubiquitous and begin to exercise impact from the moment of awareness in black infants. Imagine the vulnerability of black children to the myth of the purity of whiteness and the evil of blackness, where their dichotomies are omnipresent from birth to death. The angel is white and the devil is dark.

Herman Melville sought to extirpate the myths of the purity of whiteness and the evil of blackness.

This elusive quality it is, which causes the thought of whiteness which, divorced from more kindly associations and coupled with any object terrible in itself, to heighten that terror to the furthest bounds. Witness the white bear of the poles, and the white shark (requin) of the tropics; what but their smooth, flaky whiteness makes them the transcendent horrors they are? . . . and though in other mortal sympathies and symbolizings, this same hue (whiteness) is made the emblem of many touching, noble things—the innocence of brides, the benignity of age; though among the Red men of America the giving of the white belt of wampum was the deepest pledge of honor; though, in many climes, whiteness typifies the majesty of justice in the ermine of the Judge, and contributes to the daily state of kings and queens drawn by milk-white steeds; though even in the higher mysteries of the most august religions it has been made the symbol of the divine spotlessness and power; by the Persian fire worshippers, the white forked flame being held by the holiest on the altar; and in the Greek mythologies, Great Jove himself being made incarnate in a snow-white bull . . . yet for all these accumulated associations, with whatever is sweet, honorable, and sublime, there yet lurks an elusive something in the innermost idea of this hue, which strikes more of panic to the soul than that redness which affrights in blood.[13]

EFFECTS ON WHITES

While our concern is primarily with the effect of oppression on the objects of oppression, the oppressor is obviously also affected.

Dr. Kenneth Clark has pointed out that white children are taught the virtues of American democracy—brotherhood, equality, and justice—on one hand, but "on the other hand, they see the Negro discriminated against, rejected, segregated and humiliated. These contradictions are often taught by the same individuals and institutions who seek to socialize the child—the parents, teachers, schools and churches."[14]

In attempting to handle this conflict in their self-image, some white children "develop a personal sense of guilt; others intensify their prejudices and blame the victims of racism for their predicament; still others repress the more disturbing aspects of the conflict and assume a protective posture of moral apathy, indifference and generalized insensitivity. A pervasive cynical philosophy of 'dog-eat-dog' or 'every man for himself' may be the desperate and pathetic refuge of those unable to find a more stabilizing device in the face of the moral quandary which American racism imposes upon them."[15]

The accordance of subhuman status to black slaves by white masters had its roots not only in economic expediency but also in facets of white psychological character. Erikson has described the development of white psychological character in terms of polarities which, when counterpointed, either "left this counterpoint to a unique style of civilization, or let it disintegrate into mere contradictions."[16] The existence of such polarities as migratory versus sedentary, individualistic versus standardized, competitive versus cooperative, pious versus free thinking, and responsible versus cynical necessitates the projection of one aspect of the polarity onto others (blacks) while retaining the more salutary aspect of the polarity for the white individual. The black is then acted toward as if in fact he embodied the projected attribute.

"And even today they subsist to organize this dehumanization nationally. But I as a man of color, to the extent that it becomes possible for me to exist absolutely do not have the right to lock myself into a world of retroactive reparation."[17]

THE DEVELOPMENT OF "SOUL"

There are many aspects of the black experience that can be accounted as reactions to the effects of oppression. As previously discussed, blacks have resorted to a variety of adaptations and maladaptations in order to deal with individualized and institutionalized white racism.

Often minimized or overlooked is an aspect of the black experience that has developed in large measure independent of response
to oppression. This is "soul." "Soul is love, and it's fed by the
Southern farm and the big city ghetto. It's being flexible, spontaneous. The soul brother is sensitive and frank. He's cool, too, he judges
things by what he sees, not just by what the credentials say. Where
Black people meet, you find a special warmth that you don't find
any other place. Soul brothers can communicate by using only the
essence of a message—straight to the point. Results are more important than procedures."[18]

The soulful aspect of the black experience has resulted in a life
style and a vocabulary (verbal behavior) that are reflective of
"soul." Examples are terms such as: "burn, fox, jive, and whale."
The verbal behavior characteristic of "soul" is more than an attempt
by blacks to repudiate white, technocratic, hyper-intellectual values
and modes of expression. It is also an effort to achieve a life-sus-
taining and culture-perpetuating intimacy and affection with other
blacks.

The following letter by one of the authors underscores some of
the differences between the black experience and the white experience.

July 21, 1969

Sir:

Eldridge Cleaver's reference to Apollo 11 as a "circus to distract people's minds from the real problems which are here on the ground" is as
accurate as Spiro Agnew's statement urging America to mount an effort
to send men to Mars before the end of the century is racist and technocratic. The two men, Cleaver and Agnew, one black, the other white,
express sentiments and ideas consistent with their life experiences and
their racial identifications; the Black man says, "Let's talk about life on
earth, suffering, misery, and help our brother." The white man says in
effect, "I am a brain, not a heart or a soul. I will conquer the universe.
What do I care about suffering humanity? How much copper is there in
Biafra?"

On Wednesday. July 16th, when Apollo blasted off into infamy, a
Black woman, residing in Harlem, phoned her psychiatric social worker
to plead for help. She had no carfare to come to the hospital. Thirty
billion dollars were allocated for Neil Armstrong and Company. That
Black woman in Harlem needed twenty cents.

The emphasis on technocracy, space exploration, and unemotional
thought are consistent with a white racist orientation that equates evil

and baseness with "affective," while equating purity and honesty with "intellectual." Thus the brain rules, and the heart and "soul" are slaves. The upper stories of a building are dignified and beautified, while the cellar is dark, dirty and disdained. White is beautiful; black is evil. Thus the white Omnipotent Administrator is compelled, or driven toward intellectual excellence, while denying his "soul" of feeling life.

According to Erik Erikson, the functioning American lives with two sets of "truths": A set of religious principles or religiously pronounced political principles of a highly puritan quality, and a set of shifting slogans. Thus, the same child may have been exposed in succession or alternatively to sudden decisions expressing the slogans "Let's get the hell out of here" and again, "Let's stay and keep the bastards out."

These slogans indicate the plight of white Americans—soul versus brain. How is it resolved? By emphasizing the purity of whiteness and the filthiness of blackness? No—but by dispelling these stereotypes and dealing with earthly affairs.

Nobel Laureate Harold Urey once remarked that life is not a miracle. It is a natural phenomenon, and can be expected to appear whenever there is a planet whose conditions duplicate those of the earth. The laws of probability indicate that there must be another solar system in this infinite universe and another planet earth. Pluto, therefore, is the first step of a thousand mile journey. As the white Omnipotent Administrator thrusts further into space, he may discover another earth billions of light years away from our planet earth. Having come full circle it may then be possible to practice humanism. The "Brain" would have acquired "Soul."[19]

CONCLUSION

In this chapter the authors have reviewed the impact of oppression and racism on the behavior of blacks. Rather than viewing blacks as passive reflectors of white oppressive behavior, our emphasis has been on the extremely dynamic manner in which the black experience has evolved in response to the needs, strengths, and liabilities of blacks. Verbal behavior is a significant parameter in the black experience, and this parameter is our focus in this book.

3
The Genesis of Black American Dialects

All blacks can trace their heritage to some part of Africa. It was only as a result of the slave trade that they were dispersed throughout America and the islands of the Caribbean. But once dispersed and forced to accommodate to different alien environments, each group of blacks developed a specific language, folklore, music, and religion. These in turn influenced each group's characteristics, which in turn influenced its thinking. Each retained certain aspects of the African heritage and incorporated them with certain other aspects of the new, dominant culture. Each group of blacks reflects the dominant culture in which they were raised; hence the pronouncement "West Indians are very British." Why not? After all, they were British subjects, as the blacks in New Orleans (very French) reflect the fact that New Orleans was at one time a French territory, and so it goes. Hence also the feeling of strangeness that a West Indian newcomer, for example, gets when he arrives in Harlem and is confronted with a black culture that is in many respects alien.

Even within the United States there are strong differences between blacks from the North and blacks from the South and between poor and middle class blacks. Evidence of the latter difference is the rhetoric used at first by the black civil rights leaders who thought this guaranteed that other blacks would listen to them. But while the black leaders understood the white leaders and the white leaders understood them, the people for whom the black leaders spoke did not understand either the black or the white leaders. It took some time for those black leaders to understand the complexity of their own language. On the basis of their own emotions and

means of expressing those emotions, they were making the mistake
of believing that they were speaking for all blacks. This misconception is one source of what whites refer to as black divisiveness.

COMMON EXPERIENCES

It should be clear at this point that there are as many different
kinds of blacks as there have been environmental determinants to
affect them. But much more basic than the differences among black
subcultures are the similarities; for blacks, no matter where they
come from or what their socioeconomic status, share a basic commonality—a commonality of suffering as a result of their blackness.
This sense of suffering has been preserved in the songs, religion, and
folklore of each group of blacks; it is so universal that the songs, the
religion, and the folklore of each group contain numerous similarities.
So unmistakable are these similarities that blacks have been ascribed a universality of natural rhythm and soul. In other words, as
whites would say, "They all *sound* alike, too."

Universal black suffering may also be said to have had a major
influence in the existence of a sort of universal black language.
Even though a black Jamaican may feel an initial alienation upon
his arrival in Harlem, it does not take him long to get caught up in
the rhythms of Harlem, to pick up the slang, to feel at home with
its food and night life. The same is true for a black coming to Harlem from Africa or California or Atlanta. There is almost never
any conflict of misunderstanding over language. In fact, the shared
understanding of language may indeed lead to many of Harlem's
disturbances. It is not uncommon to visit Harlem Hospital on a busy
Saturday night and find a young man from Chicago there with
wounds inflicted by a young man from Mississippi because they
both understand the "dozens" (a word game in which close members of the family are degraded).

PRESLAVERY INFLUENCES

More provable as a basis for a universal black language than universal black suffering is the historical, factual basis of the preslavery
influences upon black English.

In order to understand the preslavery influences, it is necessary
to be aware of the medieval empire of Mali, a civilization rich in
history and culture, located in western Africa. Well over 10 percent

of black Americans can trace their ancestral home to the Mali Empire. The language of the Mali Empire was Mandingo, which is still spoken in much of western Africa. It was the first or second language of many of the first Africans to land upon American shores (before slavery), and indeed it most probably was spoken in America before any European language.

In his short monograph, *African Explorers of the New World*, Harold G. Lawrence asserts: "That Africans voyaged across the Atlantic before the era of Christopher Columbus is no recent belief. Scholars have long speculated that a great seafaring nation which sent its ships to the Americas once existed on Africa's west coast. . . . We can now state that the Mandingoes of the Mali and Songhay Empires, and possibly other Africans, crossed the Atlantic to carry on trade with the Western Hemisphere Indians and further succeeded in establishing colonies throughout the Americas."[1]

The presence of blacks with their trading masters in the time of Columbus is an even more established fact. They are represented in American sculpture and design of that period. Balboa noted the existence of black men in his passage of the Isthmus of Darien in the year 1513. And most important, Columbus reported seeing Negro traders from Guinea whose chief ware, a gold alloy called guanin, was frequently mentioned by early writers in Africa.[2]

A black form of English strongly influenced by Mandingo and other African languages became established as a trade language on the West African coast in the sixteenth century, and as the same traders who went there also went to the Americas, Mandingo and African language influence must have spread to the areas surrounding major American ports. West African scholars are known to have visited London to study English in 1554, at least ten years before William Shakespeare was born.

SLAVE PIDGIN LANGUAGE

Even before the time of slavery, at least on the west coast of Africa, pidgin English was in use in the trade centers. With the rise of slave trading centers, also on the West African coast, the use of this pidgin English became more widespread, and it is likely that at least some African slaves already knew this pidgin English when they came to the New World.

"They came in chains," Saunders Redding wrote in his book of the same title, "and they came from everywhere along the west coast of Africa—from Cape Verde and the Bights of Benin and Biafra; from Goree, Gambia, and Calabar; Anamaboe and Ambriz; the Gold, the Ivory, and the Grain Coast; and from a thousand nameless villages inland. They were, these slaves, people of at least four great races—the Negritians, the Fellatahs, the Bantus and the Gallas—and many tribes whose names make a kind of poetry: Makalolu, Bassutas, Kaffir, Koromantis; the Senegalese and the Mandingos; Ibos, Iboni, Ibani (like the parsing of a Latin verb), Efik and Fulahs, the Wysyahs and the Zandes."[3]

Out of this sea of black humanity evolved a universal black language taken from all these tribes and cultures and dialects. Ingenious indeed!

Ingeniousness notwithstanding, it could not have been otherwise. The common colonial policy was to mix slaves of various tribal origins, and thus grouped together the slaves had no choice but to adopt as their form of communication, with each other as well as with their masters, the language form most common to all of them —pidgin English. This kind of English became so well established as the principal medium of communication among black slaves in the British colonies that it was passed on to succeeding generations and became their native tongue.

An example of what New World black English may have been like in its early stages can be found in Daniel Defoe's *The Family Instructor* (London, 1715). Although the fourteen-year-old black youth, Toby, states that he was born in the New World, he speaks to his young master in pidginized English:

TOBY: Me born at Barbados.
BOY: Who lives there, Toby?
TOBY: There lives white mans, white womans, negru mans, negru womans, just so as live here.
BOY: What and not know God?
TOBY: Yes, the white man says God prayers, —no much know God.
BOY: And what do the black mans do?
TOBY: They much work, much work, —no say God prayers, not at all.
BOY: What work do they do, Toby?
TOBY: Makes the sugar, makes the ginger, —much great work, weary work, all day, all night.[4]

By the end of the seventeenth century, a pidginized form of English had become so widespread that it was the language of the coastal plantations in the Dutch colony of Surinam, in South America. An early (1718) description of the colony includes a number of examples of the local black English dialect: "Me bella well" (I am very well); "You wantee siddown pinkininne?" (Do you want to sit down for a bit?); and "You wantee go walka longa me?" (Do you want to take a walk with me?).[5] In these sentences, *wantee,* can be related to Defoe's Toby's *makee.* Also, the speaker, like Toby, uses *me* as a subject pronoun. In Toby's speech there is no example to correspond with "Me bella well," but Toby would most likely have said "Me lave at Barbados" since the *be* in his first sentence was probably a past tense marker (as it is in present-day West African pidgin English).

At least by 1776, and in all likelihood much earlier, a black dialect strikingly similar to those found in the West Indies and in Surinam existed in the southern colonies. In John Leacock's *The Fall of British Tyranny* (1776), a group of escaped slaves have boarded a British man-of-war anchored off Norfolk. The captain, Lord Kidnapper, talks to Cudjo, the leader of the group:

KIDNAPPER: Well, my brave blacks, are you come to list?
CUDJO: Eas, massa Lord, you preazee.
KIDNAPPER: How many are there of you?
CUDJO: Twenty-two, massa.
KIDNAPPER: Very well, did you all run away from your masters?
CUDJO: Massa Lord eb'ry one, me too.
KIDNAPPER: That's clever. . . . what part did you come from?
CUDJO: Disse brack, disse one, disse one, come from Hamton, disse one, disse one, come from Nawfolk, me come from Nawfolk too.
KIDNAPPER: Very well, what was your master's name?
CUDJO: Me massa name Cunney Tomsee.[6]

Although this dialect occurs in a fictional account and there may have been some alteration for the sake of color, Cudjo's dialect is very similar to the previous examples: *preazee; Me massa name.*

During the eighteenth century, the number of blacks born in the New World came to exceed the number of those brought over from Africa. Pidgin English became the mother tongue of the new generations, and in some areas it has remained so to the present day. Notable examples are the West Indian patois, the Taki-Taki of Surinam, and the Gullah spoken along the coast of South Carolina.

Gullah. Gullah is the only fairly "pure" form of pidginized English spoken in the United States today. It is the dialect of the "Geechee," a fascinating group of people who can trace their ancestry directly to Africa (even though they cannot say exactly which region). One hears of stories told by eighty-year-old men and women about mothers and fathers who "crossed the big waters" when they were young.

The Geechee are descendants of black slaves who escaped their degrading conditions on South Carolina plantations and sought refuge on the hitherto uninhabited off-shore sea islands of Johns, James, Wadamalow, Foley, and a few others. For generations they and their progeny lived relatively undisturbed, although there has long been some intercourse between the islands and the mainland. But only recently have the Geechee been identified as probably the American black man's closest remaining tie to his ancestral homeland.

Like slaves in English-speaking colonies elsewhere, those who escaped to the South Carolina Sea Islands had developed a pidginized form of English and traces similar to other pidginized English forms remain today, to a greater or lesser degree depending on the relative isolation of the island. The following religious song is a white man's song adopted by the Geechee:

> Fa-le-well Shisha Maley
> Fa-le-well en lay-vun
> Fa-le-well en lay-vun
> An shallen gane en mone
> Shisha har lepentin shu beliven
> Heaven gates are oven
> I love Shisha Maley yes Ah do
> Ah anjum biddum ena cum
> I love my Shisha yes Ah do
> Ah anjum biddum ena cum.

Very similar to the use of a reflex of English *along* in place of the English *with* in the last Surinam sentence, "You wantee go walka longa me" is the Gullah use in such sentences as "Enty you wantuh walk long me?" (Do you want to walk with me?) Some Gullah speakers still use *me* as a subject pronoun—"Me kyaan bruk-um" (I can't break it).

The old woman speaking in the next passage had experienced contact with whites all her life, but her use of pronouns was not influenced completely by standard English:

I born in 1878 the twentieth day of November. I was my ma's seventh child. Everybody run for give me name. I grow up in the white people house. I do the small thing. I could thread needle for Grandma, mon, and the make me a little dress you know. I even wash the missus' feet, that's right, sir. That's right, wash her feet in the basin. And when she was the only dressmaker round the village, she take the scrap and make a little dress for me.

My Grandma had a scarf handkerchief—a white handkerchief. She brought from Rebel Time, and when she died I tie he head with that. That's right, yes, ma'am.[7]

Creole. Thus far, only the roots of black English have been treated, and it is black English that mainly concerns us here. But there were also in America groups of slaves—those brought to the French territory of Louisiana—who had to accommodate to the French language. Like their counterparts in English-speaking colonies and territories, these slaves from different African tribes, finding themselves in a new and alien land and unable to understand either their masters or each other, began to develop a pidginized form of French—a form that, because of Louisiana's location, also contained Spanish influences. While this language was evolving, the French, who seemed from the start to have been much more interested than were the English and Americans in the slaves' attempts at linguistic accommodation, laughed at the blacks' attempts at establishing a common language in order to communicate with each other. It was thought that the Africans could never learn French well, and so there was no attempt to stop them. Although written in 1935, the following section on grammar in a paper by Edward Larocque Tinker is probably indicative of the early French attitude.

It would be impossible to describe here, for it would take an entire volume, all the myriad ways in which the tongues of African slaves mutilated and amputated the French language. There is room for only a few typical instances, but it may be taken as axiomatic that they all, without exception, made for simplification, for the Negro was as lazy of brain as he was of brawn—so lazy he always took the easiest way. Not only was he handicapped by a mentality so primitive that, to express himself at all, he had first to pare the language to its barest bones, but he was also hampered by differences of physical structure. His bulbous lips and thick tongue made it impossible for him to pronounce certain French vowel sounds. In his mouth *juge* became *jige, tortue-torti, nuit-nouitte,* and the rolled French *r* was quite beyond his powers, so he just "paid it no never-mind," said *neg'* instead of *nègre* and *vend'* for *vendre.*[8]

Obviously, Tinker never stopped to think that the slaves had not grown up with the language, and were given no opportunity to learn it in a classroom. Whatever French they learned they picked up along the way, and chiefly for the purpose of forming groups whose members understood each other sufficiently to plan an escape.

The very first theories of black dialect and language most probably dealt with the language of a group of black people who evolved *not ? known* from the intermixture of the African slaves with the French and Spanish in the New Orleans area—the Creoles.

At the time of these early theories (one of the earliest was proposed in 1885), even what to call the language was a problem. The Creoles were partly white, born of French or Spanish ancestors, and partly a mixture of African and West Indian slaves. The word *Creole* is a noun, but it is usually employed as an adjective to denote anything indigenous to Louisiana: "Creole cabbage," "Creole eggs," and so on, are accepted colloquialisms. The Creoles were proud and sensitive, and they took exception to the term *Creole dialect* because they did not want anyone to mistake their language for what was then called "Baragouin" or black jargon. One nineteenth-century scholar, Alcée Fortier, made a concession to the Creoles by calling their language the "Negro French Dialect." But this view was quickly rejected by Lafcadio Hearn, who wrote that it seemed "a slight affectation to apply to this patois the term 'Negro French' as Mr. Fortier has done—probably for the mere purpose of saving hypersensitivity; and we think so because the only reason why the patois has a great philological interest is just because it is not Negro French. Negro French exists but it is something quite different, and so long as philology the world over applies to such dialects the term 'Creole,' there is no necessity for any euphemisms. The original expression is admirably significant—as implying not only a form of language, but also the special conditions which gave the language existence."[9]

Actually, another term applied to the Creole dialect, "Gombo," seems more descriptive, if for no other reason than that it stems from Africa; Gombo (or "Gumbo") simply means mixture. The Creole dialect is derived mainly from French but also contains Spanish and African influences.

"FIELD BLACKS" AND "HOUSE BLACKS"

The Creole pride and insistence upon a distinction in terms between their language and black jargon is indicative of a phenomenon common to all groups but particularly important in relation to black language: not only does language influence psychology but also psychology influences language. In black American history, this phenomenon is best illustrated by the concept of "field and house blacks."

With the advent of the Southern plantation system as we know it, came a distinction among slaves vis-à-vis their plantation usefulness. This was usually based on color. There had been some mixing of the races before slavery was begun in the colonies, and this mixing was accelerated as the masters chose as sex objects the lighter female slaves. Since there was a need for servants in the "big house," and since those slaves with some white blood were considered superior to their darker companions, it was almost always the lighter blacks who became "house blacks." These lighter Negroes in turn grew to feel superior to the darker blacks, who were left to toil in the fields. A hostility between the two groups developed and continues among their descendants to this very day. Indeed it has to a significant degree determined the black class structure and influenced the whole psychology of black America.

Blessed with the white master's "favor," the house blacks were stimulated to "improve themselves" and to emulate the white master. They could observe at firsthand white mannerisms, white customs, and white language. In some ways, they could adopt a white mentality. Some house blacks were actively encouraged in this change and were educated; a very few even acquired wealth and freedom. The result, in terms of language, was that overt pidginizations began to disappear in favor of a more "proper" form of speech.

The field blacks, on the other hand, faced with the reality that they had not been favored by the white master and in fact had been rejected, felt the need "to be seen." Hence, the emergence of red bandannas and bright head scarfs (comparable to the bright clothes of poor blacks today). Isolated from any close contact with other than lower class white overseers and finding as his model only others of his kind, the field black settled into his behavioral and language patterns, and within the rigid boundaries of slavery the gap between himself and the house black widened. Caroline Gilman's *Recollections of a Southern Matron* contains a good illustration of the difference between a field hand dialect (Gullah) and a domestic servant dialect. Compare the gardener's "He tief one sheep—he run away las week, cause de overseer gwine for flog him" with the servant woman's "Scuse me, missii, I is giting hard o'hearing, and yes is more politer dan no."[10] At the same time the gap between the field black and the white master, despite and also because of the field black's attempts to be recognized, remained as large as ever. Obviously, a number of elements contributed to this situation, but language was chief among them for it is the most basic communicative element. No more negative or hostile feelings are engendered in a group than when it is confronted with a dialect which it considers nonstandard.

A novel written in the 1850s by a black American who had traveled extensively through the slave states shows the great contrast between an educated black man and an old "aunty":

MAN: Who was that old man who ran behind your master's horse?
AUNTY: Dat Nathan, my husban'.
MAN: Do they treat him well, aunty?
AUNTY: No, chile, wus an' any dog, da beat 'im foh little an nothin!
MAN: Is Uncle Nathan religious?
AUNTY: Yes, chile, ole man an' I's been sahvin' God dis many day, fo yeh baun! Wen any on 'em in de house git sick, den da sen for 'uncle Nathan' come pray foh dem; 'uncle Nathan' mighty good den![11]

CONCLUSION

The defeat of the South in the Civil War and the Thirteenth Amendment, freeing the slaves, ended the rigid isolation of many southern blacks. Some moved to the towns, where contact with standard English and its dialects influenced their speech. Many began to receive some sort of education and this number, prosperous and poor, increased every year. But mere contact with and education in standard English did not teach it to former slaves.

Although over the last two centuries, the proportion of black Americans speaking standard English has grown from a small group of house blacks and freedmen to hundreds of thousands, perhaps millions, of blacks, there remain at least as many and probably more who still speak a nonstandard form of English.

4
Black English as a True Language Form

When the slaves were first brought to America, they of course spoke a foreign language, just as did all later immigrant groups. And as with all the other immigrant groups, when the African slaves attempted to learn English their native languages got in the way. This "getting in the way," called "interference," refers to the tendency of individuals to make the language they are learning conform to the sound and structure of their native tongues. Polish immigrants attempting to speak English made English sound like Polish; German immigrants made English sound like German, and so on. For the African slaves, this phenomenon was compounded, because among them they spoke a number of African languages; not one but many foreign languages interfered with the development of English among slaves, and thus the dialect developed among the slaves was even more nonstandard than that of other immigrant groups.

DEVELOPMENT OF DIALECT

The slaves came into relatively little contact with whites and, as previously noted, the white linguistic models they did encounter were white overseers. It is doubtful that these men who cracked the whip were particularly articulate. In fact, the language of the white overseers was generally nonstandard as compared to that of whites in higher classes. So those linguistic models the blacks did have were poor.

During slavery, therefore, a nonstandard dialect developed in the slave subculture and every child born into that subculture learned that dialect. Lack of education and the slaves' particular isolation

38

ensured a self-perpetuating nonstandard dialect. After all, assimilation is the key to acquiring the language system of the dominant culture, as the experiences of other groups new to our shores have proven.

That is not to say that other immigrant groups have completely adopted standard English. Any country comprising people of so many different races, ethnic origins, religions, and cultural backgrounds also comprises many varieties, or dialects, of the same language. It is sometimes confusing and conflicting for members of many of these groups to understand each other, whether a cross-cultural exchange is mutually desired or forcibly experienced. But the most chaotic and confusing cross-cultural exchanges occur when blacks and whites attempt to discuss or resolve their misunderstandings. The gulf between white and black is much wider than the gulf between Irish and Jewish, for example, or between Italian and Wasp. This is so because no matter how different these other groups' religious or ethnic backgrounds may be, they are nevertheless part of the white majority and as such they speak the same cultural language. Compared to interracial differences, their intraracial differences are minimal. In contrast, the problems inherent in communication between blacks and whites seem at times to be insurmountable, for in America as in other countries interracial differences are inseparable from intercultural differences.

LANGUAGE AND CULTURE

Whenever a group of people is accorded a subjugated position in a culture, in order to survive it must band together and form a subculture. Hence, to survive in a culture that has historically ignored them, blacks have had to develop different ways of living, different ways of eating, different ways of dressing, and different modes of speaking, as a kind of code. These different ways of living and speaking evolved in the first place because of blacks' relegation to a subculture. Continued discrimination has been a chief factor in blacks' confinement to ghettos. The ghetto experience in turn perpetuates and reinforces that very subculture.

Perhaps the most defining and confining element in the ghetto subculture is language, for language produces and structures thought. The mode of thought necessary to escape the ghetto is lacking in the ghetto dweller because his language does not conform to what the white man considers proper usage. Different modes of speech produce different modes of thought; hence the inability of two groups who have different modes of speech to communicate effectively. Whites and blacks operate out of different modes of speech to the extent that the same or similar terms have entirely different meanings for the two groups. What is particularly damning for the black man is that while the linguistic deviations of other ethnic groups are seen as natural and changeable in time, the white society has invented a theory of racial inferiority to explain black language differences.

This theory is not at all warranted. It is accepted linguistic doctrine that within a large complex society where individuals from different social classes and different ethnic origins speak different dialects of the same language, one of these dialects may be considered socially more prestigious than the other and thus may be used as the standard for the nation. But this is an arbitrary, or at most a social, decision which has nothing to do with that particular dialect's linguistic merits. In other words, the dialect chosen as standard is no more highly structured, well formed, or grammatical than any of the other dialects.

Recently, considerable application of this doctrine has been made to black English, and the results have proved shocking to those whites who view black English as merely an inferior and incorrect form of standard English. Studies have shown that, far from being an arbitrary collection of bad standard English, black English is a bona fide language system with its own rules of grammar, vocabulary, and structure. In other words, as black people have known all along, there is a correct way to pronounce words and a correct grammar to be used when speaking the nonstandard black dialect. These are not contained in grammars and they are not taught in schools, but they nevertheless exist. The problem is that vocabulary, the area in which black English and standard English are most alike, masks the extent of the grammatical differences between them. Also, many simple utterances in one dialect are directly equatable with utterances in the other.

LINGUISTICS OF BLACK ENGLISH

Philologists have not as yet completely described the linguistic system of black English. Nevertheless, work has been done that has shed light on a number of different areas of the system that, taken together, indicate that there is ample reason for going on. Eventually it may be possible to formulate an entire grammar of black English and to prove thereby that black English is not merely incorrect standard English.

An illustrative consistency that operates in the black English language system is the so-called double negative, one of the chief grammatical forms seen as deviant by those people who pass judgment on the English of others. Actually, the term "double negative" is something of a misnomer, for there are many cases in standard English where double negation is quite proper:

1. He was not unaware of his surroundings.
2. There is no one who can't do it.
3. He is not without fear.

What is generally meant by the term is multiple, cumulative negation, as in "I didn't see nobody." Many speakers of white nonstandard English use the double negative and are thus branded as lower class by middle class white standard-English speakers. But generally in the case of white nonstandard-English speakers this deviation is not consistent; simple correction of a single deviation can often bring the speaker to essentially standard English.

When it comes to the kind of English spoken by socially and economically disadvantaged blacks, the situation becomes more complex, for while most of the deviations by speakers of white nonstandard English are merely haphazard or careless mistakes, the deviations in black English are deep grammatical differences.

The black English rule of negation is that a negative is attached to all negatable elements within the same simple sentence. That is, for a negative sentence to be grammatical according to the rules of black English, all indefinite pronouns, all indefinite articles, all indefinite adverbials, and the verbal auxiliary must be made negative: "Nobody ain't never met no ghost nowhere." A comparison of this sentence with its standard English equivalent shows that the difference is not simply a number of "errors" in the black English sentence. The same rule will be found operating whenever negation is necessary.[1]

Another example of black English grammar has to do with *Goes-Go* (or *Does-Do*). The commonly held opinion is that the black use of *he do* or *he go* is simply a grammatical equivalent of *he does* or *he goes,* differing only in a "dropped" ending. This is not the case, as the following sentence illustrates: "They caught the ole man 'cause he *go* around tellin' those stories all the time." Asked whether it would be acceptable to say " 'cause he *went* around tellin' . . ." the speaker rejected it because "he do it all the time." Standard English obviously does not produce sentences like "They caught the ole man because he always goes around telling lies."[2] Thus, we can see that the mere "correction" of nonstandard black English does not necessarily produce standard English.

With reference to word endings, other systematic or consistent deviations can be seen. For example, because in nonstandard black English the consonants *b, d, g, k, p,* and *t* are consistently eliminated, words like *hard* and *heart* are pronounced the same. The sound represented by the letters *th,* when it occurs at the end of a word is pronounced *f.* When it occurs at the beginning of words like *the, this, them,* and *those, d* is substituted. When it occurs in the middle of a word (*brother*), many times *d* or *v* is substituted. And because the final sounds represented by *r* in nonstandard black dialect are eliminated, *dough* and *door* are pronounced the same.

Many speakers of nonstandard black English make a grammatical and semantic distinction by means of the verb *to be:*

"He busy": He is busy (for the moment).
"He be busy": He is busy (habitually).
"He workin' ": He is working (right now).
"He be workin' ": He is working (steadily).

The grammar of standard English is unable to make such distinctions simply by means of the verb *to be.*

Some of these consistent deviations have been traced back to standard West African languages and in black history by linguists, and, doubtless, continued research will result in the tracing of other deviations. For the purpose of this discussion only a few illus-- trations need be given.

Many West African languages have a tense which is called the habitual. It is used to express action that is always occurring and it is formed with a verb that is translated as *be.* "He be coming" means something like "He's always coming," "He usually comes," or "He's been coming." It is not the same as the present tense, which is constructed without any form of the habitual *be.* The special black English use of the verb *to be* seems definitely to be a legacy of the

African slave trade, for it is found not only in American black dialect but also in the dialects of blacks far from the shores of the United States and in widely separated places. Take for example the same equivalent sentences in Gullah, Jamaican, Creole, Sranan (the Creole English of Surinam in South America), and West African pidgin English to the standard English sentence, "We were eating—and drinking, too."

Gullah: "We bin duh nyam -en' we duh drink, too."
Jamaican Creole: "We bin a nyam—an' we a drink, too."
Sranan: "We ben de nyang -en' we de gringie, too."
West African pidgin English "We bin de eat –an' we dring, too."

As mentioned previously, Gullah is considerably closer to its slave-trade heritage than are other American black dialects, but even the equivalent sentence in black nonstandard English can be related to the above sentences by the repetition of the subject *we* and the dropping of final hard consonants:

Nonstandard black English: "We was eatin'—an' we drinkin', too."[3]

Finally, look at an example of the use of *to be* by a slave in the 1830s when she asks for a permanent supply of soap: "(If) Missis only give we, we be so clean forever."[4] Compare this to the current use of *be* in nonstandard black English to denote an ongoing occurrence: "He be busy"—He is habitually busy.

The two *th* sounds of English are lacking in the West African languages; clusters of consonants are rarely found; and words are more likely to end in vowel or soft-consonant sounds rather than hard consonant sounds. *Occurrences of the Times,* an anonymous play written in 1789, provides ample documentation of the consistency in Afro-American history of the black English deviations from standard English. Debauchee, servant of a Boston master, speaks quite extensively, using *f* for a final *th* in *oaf* (oath), dropping final hard consonants in *mus* (must) and *nex* (next and substituting *t* for *th* in *tink* (think).[5]

These correspondences are much too neat to be dismissed as simply accidents. Rather, they seem to indicate that at least some of the features of American black dialects are neither skewings nor extensions of white dialect patterns, but are in fact structural vestiges of an earlier plantation Creole and ultimately of the original slave-trade pidgin English which gave rise to it.

Black English is a systematic, structured language. That is why a white person trying to speak in black dialect does not sound quite right he does not usually know its rules of pronunciation and grammar. Even if he does know the rules, he is culturally and attitudinally blinded and resistant to acknowledging their linguistical legitimacy. A case in point: white author Ambrose Gonzales, a fluent speaker of the black dialect Gullah, wrote black folktales in grammatically accurate Gullah but then described blacks who spoke the dialect as using "slovenly and careless speech."[6] In spite of his accurate recording of the dialect, his racist tendency to explain differences on the basis of inferiority caused him to conclude that the grammatical differences he observed between standard English and Gullah were due to the "characteristic laziness" of blacks rather than to the existence of the distinct grammatical system he so accurately recorded.

CONCLUSION

Many linguists are now acknowledging the legitimacy of black English as a language in its own right, and other linguists are expected to follow their lead. But this acknowledgment will have little real effect upon American blacks—or American whites—until it reaches the majority of educators involved in the education of disadvantaged black children and becomes the basis for a radically new language development program in the schools.

5
The Language of Black Children in Confrontation with Teacher Attitudes

In the classroom they made for their desks and opened their books. The name of the story they tried to read was "Come." It went:

> Come, Bill, come.
> Come with me.
> Come and see this.
> See what is here.

The first boy poked the second. "Wha' da' wor?"

"Da' wor' *is*, you dope."

"*Is?* Ain't no wor' *is*. You jivin' me? Wha' da' wor' mean?"

"Ah dunno. Jus' *is*."[1]

Perhaps the most negative aspect of the psychology of black language is illustrated by the experience of black children in the white-dominated public school system. A major goal of public education is to increase a child's social mobility and vocational success. In this it has failed with black children. And it has failed both because it has refused to see nonstandard black English as a legitimate form and because it has not developed methods to teach black children standard English. Because of this twofold failure, many black children never learn standard English in school and thus are essentially denied the economic, social, and vocational success that is the express goal of the public school system vis-à-vis its graduates.

DIALECT VERSUS STANDARD ENGLISH

Children begin to learn language long before they enter school. They learn by hearing and then imitating sounds of models. By the time they enter school, their repetition of sounds has been arranged in patterns and they have internalized the basic features of the particular variety of language in their primary cultural, usually home, environment. To them, it is the "right" way to talk; in fact, "rightness" and "wrongness" do not enter into it—it is the only way they and everyone else around them speak.

When black children come to school speaking the nonstandard black dialect, however, they are usually told, "You can't speak that way," or, "Don't use that language," and this criticism continues practically unabated throughout their years in school. Language is an identity label, a reflection and badge of one's culture; criticism of an individual's speech is thus really a criticism of his culture and all those who share it. Such criticism, coming as it does from an awesome authority figure such as a teacher, is not likely to enhance a small child's self-concept. In addition, from the child's viewpoint, the criticism is unfounded. The children know very well that they can talk "that way" and, furthermore, that they are understood by each other and by everyone else in their primary cultural environment. Their parents, neighbors, friends, relatives, and almost everyone else except the teachers at school talk "that way."

DIALECT AND COGNITIVE DEVELOPMENT

The teachers, however, have the power where the children's schooling is concerned. It is they who often see black children's nonstandard dialect as a reflection of inadequate cognitive development. Because the nonstandard dialect the children speak is *different* from standard English, it is automatically assumed to be *inferior*, and since language is essential to cognition, it is thought that an inferior language must impair cognitive development of those who speak it. This point of view is supported by all sorts of research data, often based on the results of tests for cognitive development.

Both the point of view and its bases are erroneous, however. When tested for cognitive development, black children are given tasks which require cognitive skills and development derived from a white middle class experience. Thus they fail these tasks, causing many testers and teachers to assume wrongly that they are inferior or deficient in cognitive development. Perhaps these teachers would understand the problem better if they took the following test, keyed to *non-white, lower class culture*.

THE DOVE COUNTERBALANCE INTELLIGENCE TEST

If you score less than 20 (67 percent) on the test, you are virtually failing by Yale standards, and might therefore conclude that you have a low ghetto I.Q. As white middle class educators put it, you are "culturally deprived." Who knows, perhaps OEO will fund a program in remedial education for you.

1. What instrument did "T-Bone Walker" play? (a) trombone (b) piano (c) "T" flute (d) guitar (e) "hambone."

2. In the famous blues legend, who did "Stagger Lee" kill? (a) his mother (b) Frankie (c) Johnny (d) his girlfriend (e) Billy.

3. A "gas head" is a person who has a _____. (a) fast-moving car (b) stable of one "lace" (c) "process" (d) habit of stealing cars (e) long jail record for arson.

4. If a man is called a "blood," then he is a' _____. (a) fighter (b) Mexican-American (c) Negro (d) hungry hemophile (e) Redman or Indian.

5. If you throw the dice and seven is showing on top, what is facing down? (a) seven (b) snake eyes (c) boxcars (d) little joes (e) eleven.

6. Jazz pianist Ahmad Jamal took an Arabic name after becoming famous. Previously, he had some fame with what he called his slave name. What was his previous name? (a) Willie Lee Jackson (b) LeRoi Jones (c) Wilbur McDougal (d) Fritz Jones (e) Andy Johnson.

7. What does "C. C." mean in "C. C. Rider"? (a) civil service (b) church council (c) country circuit preacher or an old time rambler (d) country club (e) Cheatin' Charlie (the Boxcar Gunsel).

8. Cheap "chitlings" (not the kind you buy at the frozen food counter) will taste rubbery unless they are cooked long enough. How soon can you stop cooking to eat and enjoy them? (a) 15 minutes (b) 2 hours (c) 24 hours (d) 1 week (on low flame) (e) 1 hour.

9. "Down home" (the South), what is the average daily earning (take home) for the average "soul brother" who is picking cotton (in season from sun up to sun down)? (a) 75¢ (b) $1.65 (c) $3.50 (d) $5.00 (e) $00.00.

10. If a judge finds you guilty of "holding weed" in California,

what is the most he can give you? (a) indeterminate (b) a nickel (c) a dime (d) a year in the county jail (e) $00.00

11. "Bird" or "Yardbird" was the jacket that jazz lovers from coast to coast hung on _____. (a) Lester Young (b) Peggy Lee (c) Benny Goodman (d) Charlie Parker (e) "Birdman of Alcatraz."

12. A "hype" is a person who _____. (a) always says he feels sickly (b) has water on the brain (c) uses heroin (d) is always ripping and running (e) is always sick.

13. Hattie Mae Johnson is on the county. She has four children and her husband is now in jail for non-support, as he was unemployed and not able to give her money. Her welfare check is now $286.00 per month. Last night she went out with the biggest player in town. If she got pregnant, then nine months from now, how much more will her welfare check be? (a) $80.00 (b) $2.00 (c) $35.00 (d) $150.00 (e) $100.00.

14. "Hully Gully" came from _____. (a) East Oakland (b) Fillmore (c) Watts (d) Harlem (e) Motor City.

15. What is Willie Mae's last name? (a) Schwartz (b) Matauda (c) Gomez (d) Turner (e) O'Flaherty.

16. The opposite of square is _____. (a) round (b) up (c) down (d) hip (e) lame.

17. Do the Beatles have SOUL? (a) yes (b) no (c) maybe.

18. A "handkerchief head" is _____. (a) a cool cat (b) a porter (c) an "Uncle Tom" (d) a hoddi (e) a preacher.

19. What are the "Dixie Hummingbirds?" (a) a part of the K.K.K. (b) a swamp disease (c) a modern gospel group (d) a Mississippi Negro para-military strike force (e) deacons.

20. "Jet" is _____. (a) an East Oakland motorcycle club (b) one of the gangs in *West Side Story* (c) a news and gossip magazine (d) a way of life for the very rich.

21. "Tell it like it _____." (a) thinks I am (b) baby (c) try (d) is (e) y'all.

22. "You've got to get up early in the morning if you want to _____." (a) catch the worms (b) be healthy, wealthy, and wise (c) try to fool me (d) fare well (e) be the first one on the street.

23. And Jesus said, "Walk together children _____." (Cor. 3:3) (a) don't you get weary. There's a great camp meeting (b) for we shall overcome (c) for the family that walks together talks together (d) by your patience you will win your souls

(e) find the things that are above, not the things that are on Earth.

24. "Money don't get everything it's true— _____. (a) but I don't have none and so I'm blue (b) but what it don't get I can't use (c) so make with what you've got (d) but I don't know that and neither do you.

25. "Bo-Diddley" is a _____. (a) game for children (b) cheap wine (c) singer (d) new dance (e) Mojo call.

26. Which word is most out of place here? (a) splib (b) blood (c) grey (d) spook (e) black.

27. How much does a short dog cost? (a) 15¢ (b) $2.00 (c) $0.35 (d) 5¢ (e) 86¢ + tax.

28. A "pimp" is also a young man who lays around all day. (a) true (b) false.

29. If a pimp is up tight with a woman who gets state aid, what does he mean when he talks about "Mother's Day"? (a) second Sunday in June (b) third Sunday in June (c) first of every month (d) first and fifteenth of every month (e) none of these.

30. Many people would say that "Juneteenth" (June 19) should be made a legal holiday because this was the day when _____. (a) the slaves were freed in the U.S.A. (b) the slaves were freed in Texas (c) the slaves were freed in Jamaica (d) the slaves were freed in California (e) Martin Luther King, Jr. was born (f) Booker T. Washington died.

(Answers in back of book, page 75).

Frequently, on the basis of standard tests, black children with normal cognitive development are placed in classes for "slow" children, thus hindering future normal cognitive development.

DIALECT AND SPEECH DEVELOPMENT

An even more common false assumption is that disadvantaged black children are nonverbal. This means that their language is incomplete and implies inferiority. In some cases this "nonverbal" label applies: that is, to those severely disadvantaged black children who suffer from poor health, malnutrition, emotional instability, or physical disorders. In such cases language development and the employment of language *is* restricted. But too often no distinction is made between these children and children who do not suffer from the above afflictions. The majority of disadvantaged black children are not restricted in their language development and their language employment, nor do they have a language disorder in the physical sense. The label "nonverbal" is applied to them simply because they do not use standard English and because of the results of attitudes toward their language.

When disadvantaged black children enter school, most are as talkative as other children; but from the time they enter school they are corrected in their speech. The effect of this constant correction is the shutting off of speech at a crucial time in the children's language development. In the primary grades, language is still in the formative process and it is important for young children to express their ideas, to interact with the environment, the teacher, and each other while using the language system they can best use. Continual correction causes them to speak less and less. Thus, instead of reinforcing the child's primary language, as it does with that of middle class children, the school not only does not reinforce the black child's primary language but actually retards the use of the language per se by the child. Reading ability is particularly handicapped, for the children are required to read words containing sounds that are either lacking in their auditory repertoires or are in conflict with the phonetics of their dialect. In other words, while the middle class student goes to school and learns to read the language he speaks, the disadvantaged black student is learning to read a foreign language. In later grades, much of the discussion in the classroom concerns issues and topics that are not relevant to the needs, interests, or backgrounds of disadvantaged black children. Therefore, black children are reluctant to take part in classroom discussions and so are labeled "nonverbal."

The error of this labeling should be obvious to anyone who observes disadvantaged black children outside the classroom. In every other situation they are highly verbal. Like all other young children they make up jingles and rhymes to accompany games. More than most other children, they engage in verbal bantering, the skillful and humorous use of language to "put down" another person or members of his family. The most highly developed form of verbal bantering in the black subculture (and exclusive to it) is "playing the dozens." Playing the dozens is to talk about another person's mother (or other female family member) either in an insulting or humorous manner, depending upon the speaker's purpose. The object is to use language cleverly, more cleverly than one's opponent.

H. "Rap" Brown received his nickname because of his skill at playing the dozens, as the following example shows:

> I fucked your mama
> Till she went blind.
> Her breath smells bad,
> But she sure can grind.
>
> I fucked your mama
> For a solid hour.
> Baby came out
> Screaming, Black Power.
>
> Elephant and the Baboon
> Learning to screw.
> Baby came out looking
> Like Spiro Agnew.[2]

A more humane form of verbal bantering is "signifying," a term that has many meanings. It is, again, the clever and humorous use of words, but it can be used for many purposes—"putting down" another person, making another person feel better, or simply expressing one's own feelings. To quote H. Rap Brown once more:

> Man, I can't win for losing.
> If it wasn't for bad luck, I wouldn't have no luck at all.
> I been having buzzard luck
> Can't kill nothing and won't nothing die
> I'm living on the welfare and things is stormy
> They borrowing their shit from the Salvation Army
> But things bount to get better 'cause they can't get no worse.
> I'm just like the blind man, standing by a broken window
> I don't feel no pain.
> But it's your world
> You the man I pay rent to
> If I had your hands I'd give 'way both my arms.
> Cause I could do without them
> I'm the man but you the main man
> I read the books you write
> You set the pace in the race I run
> Why, you always in good form
> You got more foam than Alka Seltzer. . . .[3]

Most black children (especially males) participate in these forms of verbal bantering, and they are highly verbal forms. They illustrate the fact that disadvantaged children are not "nonverbal." They are only verbally different.

In addition, it would behoove teachers of black children—and probably surprise most black people—to know that the verbal bantering common to the black subculture is a direct carry-over from Africa. Lyrical lampooning was an African custom highly regarded in preslavery days. All the African kings had in their entourage men who functioned in much the same way as the court jesters of the Middle Ages. They had a highly developed ability to improvise songs, particularly of a satirical form; in the space of a few verses they could exalt a man to the sky or reduce him to dirt. Subjects suing for royal favor would bribe these bards to sing their praises, or at least to abstain from ridiculing them. The bards wielded great power, but they were so hated that when they died they were denied the right of burial and their bodies were thrown into hollow trees to rot.[4]

EFFECTS OF TEACHER ATTITUDES

When educators label black children "nonverbal" they set off a chain of events that is called a "self-fulfilling prophecy." The children are labeled "nonverbal"; teacher expectation is thus lowered; and the children's performance conforms to teacher expectation. Children tend to achieve at the level teachers expect them to achieve. Hence, disadvantaged black children never learn standard English and are denied access to academic achievement, social mobility, and vocational success. Because their form of English is seen as inferior, and repeated correction does not result in their learning standard English, they are assumed to be retarded in cognitive development and are not expected to achieve. So much for academic achievement. Because they do not learn standard English and because their nonstandard form of English, and thus *they,* are seen as inferior by those who speak standard English, they are denied social mobility. Because they do not learn standard English, they are automatically disqualified for many good jobs, particularly those involving contact with the public either face-to-face or over the telephone, even though they may be qualified in every other way. So much for vocational success. Black language perpetuates the ghetto.

CONCLUSION

Although teachers have the most direct contact and thus the most direct influence upon disadvantaged black children's failure in school and failure to learn standard English, teachers are not entirely to blame for their attitudes. They have been trained to hold these attitudes. Also, educational literature is filled with negative descriptions of the language of disadvantaged black children. Teacher attitudes are also culturally determined. While they are well aware that Spanish, German, or Swahili has a grammar different from that of English, everything in our culture has conditioned them to regard black English as anything but a linguistic system in its own right. Even if, on his own, a teacher has become aware that black children are systematic in their deviations from standard English and has realized that constant correction will not result in their learning standard English, he has little precedent to follow in finding how to deal effectively with the problem. In order to correct the problem, a majority of linguists and educators must first recognize that black English is in fact a language by itself, departing systematically from standard English. Then, these educators and linguists must change the traditional language program from one that treats black English as a deviation to one that concentrates upon teaching standard English as a second languge—not one that is superior to black English, but one that is necessary to know and use in certain situations, such as job interviews, work environments, and social gatherings, when one must function in the dominant culture where standard English is the dialect that is used for communication.

At present, programs to teach standard English exist, but they are few and they are experimental. They must become the accepted norm before disadvantaged black children begin to show their inherent learning potential within the context of the existing public school system, and before the solid wall of the ghetto will begin to show cracks.

6
America's Debt to the Language of Black Americans

It would be ideal if, simultaneously with the recognition by white standard-English speakers of the legitimacy of black English and the learning of standard English by disadvantaged black children, there were to be a recognition by white America of its debt to the language of black Americans. Particularly in the area of informal language, this debt is great; but it is also considerable in literature and music and, to a certain extent, perhaps, also in the actual thought processes of white America. Such a recognition should not be difficult; one need only listen to American slang, for example, to know that it is largely black slang. One need only realize that in a situation where two different groups experience prolonged close sociocultural contact there is bound to be not only conflict but also cultural exchange. Arguments stressing the dominant position of whites and the subcultural and thus non-influential (upon whites) existence of blacks have no factual basis. Even a casual investigation into any analogous historical situation should reveal, as Wilhelm Reich has pointed out, that a subculture always has a proportionately larger impact upon a dominant culture than vice versa.

Many of the black language influences upon the American language have gone unrecognized because they have been slow and subtle. Many also have gone unrecognized because they were originally introduced by whites as conscious imitations of blacks to achieve humor or local color. The fact that in many cases these influences remained on their own terms is not acknowledged. This section will treat a few examples in the areas of literature, music, and informal language.

DRAMA

Black dialects early found their way into American literature, much earlier than the nineteenth-century local-color movement, erroneously considered by many to have produced the first extensive use in writing of American black language. As early as 1721, Cotton Mather had recorded three words of the black dialect: *grondy* (many); *cutty* (skin); and *sicky* (sick). And about 1782 Benjamin Franklin inserted four or five lines of black dialect into his tract "Information to Those Who Would Remove to America."[1]

But it is in American drama that the black dialect first comes to the fore with any regularity or relevance. At least ten plays written before 1800 show this influence. The dialect in these plays was not written according to any literary tradition or formula. There can be little doubt that most of the black characters were drawn from life and that their speech is a crude, occasionally distorted, duplication of the sounds which the playwrights thought they had heard. There is very little consistency of spelling or syntax, even within the same play, but such variations are understandable. No until much later did written black dialect assume literary conventionality. And uniformity was genuinely impossible in the eighteenth century; many slaves had only recently been brought from Africa and were struggling to learn English despite the interferences that their various languages produced.

According to Arthur Hobson Quinn, the first black character in American drama is the servant Ralpho in Robert Munford's comedy of elections in Virginia, *The Candidates* (written 1770, published 1798).[2] Ralpho does not speak in dialect (evidently), but his music of multisyllabic words would become typical of the comic black of later drama. "Gadso!" he says, "This figure of mine is not reconsiderable in its delurements, and when I'm dressed out like a gentleman, the girls, I'm thinking, will find me desistible."

The first positive use of black dialect in American drama was probably an anonymous play entitled *The Trial of Atticus, before Justice Beau, for a Rape* (1771). Caesar, a black comic, makes a brief appearance at the trial:

JUSTICE: Well, *Caesar*, did Mrs. Chuckle ever tell you anything about *Atticus'* abusing of her?

CAESAR: Yesa, Maser, *he* tell me that *Atticus* he went to bus 'em one day, and shilde [child] cry, and so he let 'em alone.

JUSTICE: How came she tell you of this?
CAESAR: Cause, Maser, I bus *him* myself.[3]

The author of the play considered Caesar's substituting the masculine for the feminine pronoun when referring to Mrs. Chuckle odd enough to be italicized, a fact that is helpful in tracing various features of black English in history.

Extensive use of black dialect is evident in the play *Occurrences of the Times,* written in 1789. Following is a typical speech by the black Debauchee, about a duel that did not take place:

Ah! dat is—we didn't fite—twixt you and I, massa he no courage. Misser *Harcourt* he say—shentlemen preas to measus; and my massa say— shentlemen you no de law.[4]

Although the playwright took little care to render the dialect consistently (*assassinate* is written as *cisnate* in one passage and as *fascinate* in another), Debauchee's speech is quite convincing, and indeed, the playwright was quite faithful to a number of dialectical rules.

Some playwrights and other writers eventually brought black dialect to the point of near-unintelligibility. Samuel Low's *The Politician Out-witted* (written in 1788) is an example. When Humphrey offers to help his servant carry a trunk, Cuffy replies:

Tankee, massa buckaraw; you gi me lilly lif, me bery glad; —disa ting damma heby. (Puts down the trunk.) —An de debelis crooka tone ina treet more worsa naw pricka pear for poor son a bitch foot; and de cole pinch um so too![5]

As this is the only speech Cuffy makes, it is clear that Low employed the use of dialect purely for color—a very self-conscious device.

Despite the exaggerations, the oddities of spelling not warranted by the spoken language (e.g., *fite* for *fight*), and the comic intentions which caused the playwrights to overcolor the language in order to provide humor, these early dramatic efforts represent the first consistent attempts to translate the spoken sounds and sentences into written words. They mark the beginning of a literature of black dialect which eventually was to become characteristic of much of the best native American writing. When the local-color movement— the first truly American literary trend—arose in the nineteenth century, black life, black folklore, and most of all black dialect were major and determining aspects.

White writers have borrowed heavily from black folklore. Gombo stories like the following are the source of Joel Chandler Harris's "Brer Rabbit" stories.

Before every Gombo story there was a ritual. The black narrator would call out "Bonne foi! Bonne foi!" in order to attract attention and give some validity to his story. The listeners would then answer in unison, "Lapin! Lapin!" to show they were just as smart as the storyteller and indeed would take the story with a grain of salt. Then the storyteller would launch into some tale like that of Compair Bouki (Friend Goat), who fired up his kettle and began to sing to attract the macaques (monkeys). After the simian tribe had gathered, Compair Bouki said, "I'm goint to jump in the kettle, and when I say 'I'm cooked,' take me out." They did as he ordered, but when the monkeys' turn came and they jumped into the pot and then asked to be taken out, Compair Bouki replied ironically, "If you were cooked, you wouldn't be able to say so." Only one little monkey escaped. Then Bouki tried the same trick with another group of monkeys. But the first little monkey had warned his kind, so when the goat, expecting to be taken out, said "I'm cooked," the macaques left him in the pot and chanted gleefully, "If you were cooked, you wouldn't be able to say so."[6]

The relation of this tale to the "Brer Rabbit" stories is obvious, as is its relation to African stories like that of Minaba, a young girl who lived with her mother and two sisters in a poor village where there was little meat to be had. One day, after struggling to place a full bucket of water upon her head, she accepted the assistance of a kuku, a monkey-like animal, who had come to the water pipe to drink. Thinking how sweet and tender the kuku would be to eat but not wanting to share the food with her sisters, Minaba later sneaked back to the spot where she had met the kuku and killed it with her bow and arrow. Her sisters were angry with her when she returned with her prize. When the kuku was ready to be cooked, Minaba asked her sisters to help her prepare the pot and cook him, but the dead kuku sang, "Let Minaba cook the food alone because when Minaba came to the pipe I was the one who helped her," and the sisters refused. When the kuku was cooked, the sisters declined to join Minaba in eating the meat, saying, "Eat it yourself," and so Minaba ate the whole thing by herself. In a little while, Minaba began to feel sick and she asked her sisters to take her to a cool, shady place in the forest where she could lie down. But before the sisters could respond, the kuku inside Minaba's stomach began to sing, "Let Minaba go alone because when Minaba went to the pipe I was the one who helped her." Minaba had to go to the forest alone. She rolled on the ground in pain, and then suddenly the kuku ran out of Minaba's mouth and Minaba lay still, dead.[7]

The preceding stories show a worldly-wise understanding of character. At the same time they manage to relate to class consciousness and to make shrewd and exact observations of situations. Their appeal is great and they have exercised considerable influence upon American writers. The greatest tribute, perhaps, has been paid by Ambrose Gonzales, who not only wrote folktales after the manner of Gullah folktales but also wrote them in perfect Gullah dialect.

WHITE SOUTHERN SPEECH

In order to acquire the intimate knowledge of the black idioms and dialects which they so skillfully use, both Gonzales and Harris must have experienced them at firsthand for some time, probably since childhood.[8] Such experience was not at all uncommon in the South and indeed seems to have been sufficiently widespread to constitute another example of the influence of the black dialect upon standard English, at least southern standard English.

In 1746, G. L. Campbell, a British traveler to the American colonies, wrote of the southern white planters: "One thing they are very faulty in, with regard to their Children, which is, that when young, they suffer them too much to prowl amongst the young Negroes, which insensibly causes them to imbibe their manner and broken speech."[9]

In 1908, describing the Charlestonian aristocracy of his day, John Bennett wrote: "It is true that, up to the age of four, approximately, the children of the best families, even in town, are apt to speak an almost unmodified Gullah, caught from brown playmates and country bred nurses; but at that age the refinement of cultivation begins, and "the flowers o' the forest are a' weed awa!"[10]

A fairly common opinion is that Gullah is a dying dialect, now limited to the Carolina Sea Islands. There is abundant evidence, however, that it or a transitional dialect based on it, is still widely spoken, even in metropolitan Charleston, and even by some whites. It is useless to argue that it is natural for children to pick up the language but that once they reach adolescence they are immune to further influence.

Today, social conditions are such that communication between black and white children is not so intimate as it was in the days of plantation and plantation-like life. Nevertheless, those black dialect words and forms that the white children did imbibe in those days, though weakened through time, must still be assumed to exert an influence in the speech of whites in the onetime plantation areas.

SLANG

The vital and increasing influence of black words and forms upon American slang need not be assumed. It obviously exists in the speech of those whites who "dig" jazz, in that of whites who are associated with those who "dig" jazz, and in that of those young whites disillusioned with the dominant American culture who have absorbed the language of the black subculture. This language has been used by the young both as a defense mechanism and as an articulation of the revolutionary spirit, reasons that stand in sharp contrast to the original, slanderous imitation of the slaves' speech by white slaveholders or the "black-face" "black-talk" of white minstrels. Of course, vestiges of the original smirking use remain, but in most instances the usage is open, respectful, and conscious of the alternatives to the dominant culture intrinsic in black life and black language. But more important than this influence are the unconscious uses of black slang throughout the country and the open, conscious imitation of blacks. A list of some of these words and terms appears in the back of this book; for the purposes of this argument, only a few will be treated here.

Perhaps the most widely used slang form traceable to black origins is the term *O.K.* Attempts to trace the term to English, German, French, Finnish, Greek, and Choctaw sources have met with little success. *O.K.* can be shown to derive from similar expressions in a number of African languages and to have been used in black Jamaican English more than twenty years before its use by whites in New England.[11]

Some of the other "Americanisms" that appear to have an African or probably African origin are *jazz, jitter* and *jitter-bug, hep* (or *hip*), *banjo, boogie-woogie, jam* (as in *jam session*), *jive, to goose, to bug someone, to lam* (go), *to dig* (to understand or appreciate), *uh-huh* and *uh-uh* (for yes and no), *ofay* and *honkie* (names for the white man), *cocktail, guy*, and *bogus*. Many such words are direct-loan words from Africa; others are metamorphosed African words; and still others are direct translations.

Among the most interesting forms are those that express concepts oppositioned to the standard English usage: such as *bad* meaning good; *hard* having a positive connotation; *kill* to mean affect strongly, to fascinate; *love letter* to mean a bullet; and *murder* to express approval of something excellent. The source of these forms is not African; it is distinctly Afro-American, born of the need of blacks to change or "negate" the negative concept of blackness.[12]

MUSIC

Black jazz musicians were chiefly responsible for many black language influences upon American slang. They originated the vernacular of what is perhaps the most original and revolutionary art form in North America.

Black music per se may be said to occupy that unique position. The United States consumes a great deal of music, but as yet has not produced nearly so much as it consumes. Unlike most other nations, it does not have a wealth of native music. The only native music it can boast is black music, but America has not yet accepted that simple truth. Black music is the closest America has to folk music and as such black music is—or should be—as important to American musical culture as it is to the spiritual existence of blacks.

There are three types of black music: folk, popular, and classical.

Folk Music. Folk music is produced without formal musical training; it is an emotional creation born out of deep suffering and its spiritual compensation in intense religious feeling. Black folk music comprises the spirituals. It evolved on the plantation, and because the plantation was far from theaters, music halls, and other sources of entertainment, it was encouraged by the whites. Through their blacks, the whites had entertainment, and black folk music thereby seeped into the skins of the southern aristocrats.

Popular Music. Popular black music is the black man's own

natural return to gaiety and humor informed by sorrow and serious-
ness. For a long time this music was confined chiefly to the black
community. However, in the years since World War II, with the
recording business boom, popular black music has become popular
American music. Black performers or white performers whose style
is imitative of black styles head record-rating charts, and it is clear
that if it were not for black popular music there would have been
no such phenomenon in American musical culture.

Jazz. The third, or classical, type of black music is contemporary
classical jazz, a derivation of the spiritual and folklore form, as is,
for that matter, popular black music. Jazz is the child of an urban
experience, while blues is that of a rural experience. As George Cain
puts it in his novel *Blueschild Baby,* "Jazz is the city, only city
niggers can feel this thing. I never liked it much, never listened
really, hadn't been here long enough. To my country ear it was mad
noise. But I'm a part of the tremendous pressure that generates that
sound and I feel it so good now. Jazz is the black man's history."[13]

Or as Cecil Taylor says about his music in the liner notes of his
Looking Ahead, "Everything I've lived, I am."[14] Music, like religion,
is very much a part of the psychology of blacks in America. Like
religion, it is black people's own special brand of worship and style,
contributing much to the black man's perception and self-esteem.

But although it is a product of the unique black experience,
jazz is also universal. Langston Hughes found this in his travels:
"Everywhere, around the world," he noted in *I Wonder As I
Wander,* "folks are attracted by American jazz. A good old Dixie-
land stomp can break down almost any language barriers, and
there is something about Louis Armstrong's horn that creates
spontaneous friendships."[15] This universality is intensified when jazz
is analyzed in terms of its impact upon America. Increasingly
urbanized, pervaded by the tension of a fast, ever-changing society,
subject to "future shock," America in its entirety reverberates to
the sound of jazz. Jazz—black jazz—is the expression of America.

The popularity of black music does not of course extend equally
to all segments of American society. It applies chiefly to urbanized
Americans, to rebellious Americans, and to young Americans in
whom can be found at its greatest heights, the tension of America.
It is for these people that the black musician and black music
speak the truth. The musician and his music represent a breaking

away from tradition and a turning to a new vision. They symbolize rebellion, and, at the same time change, at their heights. For urbanized Americans they are musical translations of life as well as means of escape from life. For rebellious Americans and for American youth, they are "underground" forms of communicating, and means by which to gain access to the black (real feeling and living) experience.

"Communication" is the important word here. Before man "advanced" to the literal stage, he lived in cultures where feelings were purely feelings and labels for them were not necessary. And it seems that today we may be finding our literal culture evolving back to an essentially nonliteral one; witness the rock culture, in which noise and sounds seem to be enough to transmit the message of the "youth culture" to youth, and the thousands of sensitivity groups springing up around the country that emphasize touching as a chief means of communication. Perhaps because blacks in America have historically been thwarted in communicating verbally or literally, jazz is essentially nonverbal communication, on an emotional level. This is a kind of communication increasingly sought by alienated Americans. It has wedged itself deeply into the sensibility of black Americans, but also it has become more than ever before an extension of young or rebellious white persons' *conscious* communication apparatus.

CONCLUSION

Black language has exerted a strong influence upon the literature, informal language, and music of white America, not to mention the actual psyche of white America. It would behoove white America to realize this influence if it is ever in mature awareness to know itself.

7
Black Language
for Survival

And finally we arrive at the most basic phenomenon and determinant of black language—survival. The historic reluctance, if not outright refusal, of whites to recognize black English as anything but incorrect standard English has blinded them to the ways in which blacks have historically used both Africanisms and language forms borrowed or adopted from their white masters in order to deceive or make fun of their masters, to communicate secretly with each other, and to plan revolts and methods of escape.

There are theories that what whites consider simply poor grammatical usage by blacks actually evolved for a definite purpose. One example is the double negative, which might be traced to the African language rule that in a negative sentence ("I didn't see nobody nowhere") all the elements are negated. It is very possible that black slaves discovered the deceptive possibilities in the use of the double negative. "I didn't see nobody nowhere" can mean "I saw somebody somewhere."

This use of the double negative is hypothesized; other deceptive uses of language are not only probable but necessary. Otherwise, how could the slaves, guarded and watched as closely as they were, have engaged in so much communication with each other or kept so much information from their masters? Of course, many white masters did not think their slaves capable of deception and withholding information. Lydia Parrish, who spent years studying the black people of the Georgia Sea Islands, wrote: "It is amusing to question Southerners as to the number of times they remember hearing Negroes volunteer information. Not one so far has recalled an instance in which something has been told that was not common knowledge."[1]

It did not take the black slaves long to understand that whatever they said, to their white masters or even to each other, must be couched in words with double meanings, in half truths, and in other forms that would ensure their own safety, and they quickly became adept at such verbal survival mechanisms.

A child calls to its mother, "O Mamma look dat da fulafafa!" The mother answers with a superior air, "Gal you bin in dis buckle country (buckra is white man) so long an' you can't say walisapapa." "Fulafafa" and "walisapapa" both mean woodpecker in an African dialect,[2] and it is fairly common knowledge that southern blacks have for a long time referred to southern whites as peckerwood.

PROVERBS

The necessity for subtlety and deception probably also influenced the prolific production of black folklore, although, as the Minaba story in Chapter 6 shows, African folklore was prolific in itself and constituted the chief basis for black American folklore. The same is true of the relationship between African and black American proverbs.

Lydia Parrish cites several examples of this relationship. She once asked a black man named Joe what to do about a certain singer who continually doublecrossed his group, and Joe answered, "My ole gran mother use t' say: 'Them's the kind you gotta feed with a long spoon.' " Mrs. Parrish notes the similarity between this proverb and the Surinam or Dutch Guianean, "When you eat with the devil then you must have a long fork." Another time she heard a black preacher tell his congregation that when a man dug a pit for his neighbor, at the same time he dug one for himself. Another Surinam proverb states, "When a person digs a hole to put another in he himself falls into it."[3]

Proverbs have been called "the wisdom of many and the wit of one." They can also be called "the wisdom of nations." This is true particularly in the case of blacks. Despite all the deprivation and suffering they experienced, they nevertheless handed down the fruits of their experience through proverbs and other forms of folklore which, as the above examples show, are relatively intact.

Today we call the use of such proverbs by black people "mother wit," but let us not forget the survival value of such proverbs. The advantage of proverbs is their indirection. They allow no accusation to be made against the speaker, and yet their whimsical humor is more telling than any literal presentation of facts. In short, for the slaves, as well as for all black Americans historically, it was best to convey an idea by inference rather than to state it directly.

J. Mason Brewer compiled an extensive collection of folklore in his *American Negro Folklore*. The following proverbs are a tiny fraction of those he collected. However, they exemplify black Americans' fantastic ability to convey ideas indirectly but humorously:

Mule don't see w'at his naber doin'.

Dogs don't bite at de front gate.

One-eyed mule can't be handled on de bline side.

Youk'n hide de fier, but w'at you gwine do wid de smoke?

Yistidday kin take keer ob itse'f.

You can't tell much 'bout a chicken-pie tell you git froo de crus'.

Fiel' mouse lay still when de sparrer-hawk sail.

De mousetrap don't go to sleep.

De old steer gits s'picious when dey feed him too high.

De old rabbit thinks 'speriunce cost too much when you git it fum a mash-trap.

Old Satun mus' be a silent pardner in de ownership o' some folks.

Rabbit know a fox track same as a houn'.

Heap o' people rickerlec' favors by markin' 'em down in de snow.

'Tain't no countin' on de notions ob a grav'-vine nor de chune ob a mockin'-bird.

De crab-grass b'lebes in polertics.

Fish-trap don't make no noise, but it do good work.

Don' say no mo' wid yo' mouf dan yo' back kin stan'.[4]

These proverbs exemplify the black sense of humor, which may truly be said to be the factor most responsible for black survival, first under slavery and later under the yoke of second-class citizenship. No matter what the situation, black humor shines through. One case was recorded at Washington's crossing of the Delaware, where it is said that one of the blacks with Washington yelled out, "Mr. British General, you am Cornwallis, but I'se going now to change your name to Cobwallis, for General Washington, with us colored pussons, has shelled all the corn offen you!"[5]

STORIES

Black American stories further illustrate black humor as the ability to say much in a few words. It can be definitely said that black people have historically used stories to teach their children, particularly those who received scanty formal training, as well as to convey ideas safely.

The following tale is from the store of Moses Miles, who could neither read nor write and who had never traveled more than a hundred miles from the plantation near Tallahassee where he lived. He had never heard of Joel Chandler Harris and firmly believed that he had created all the animal stories he knew:

Eyeball Candy

Buh Fox came along one day. Buh Rabbit had just little round ball candy. He called it eyeball candy. He come on up dere where Buh Fox was.

Buh Fox, he said, "Buh Rabbit!"

He said, "Uh hun."

"What dat you eatin'?"

"Oh, man, dis somp'un good. You wanna taste it?"

"Yeah! I wanna taste it."

So he let him taste a piece of the candy. And Buh Fox taste it.

He say, "What you call it?"

"Eyeball candy."

He said, "Reckon if I pull out one of my eyes, it'd eat like dis?"

He said, "Oh, man, yeah! yeah! It'd eat like dat, sho!"

So he let Buh Rabbit pull one of his eyeballs out. Buh Rabbit took some of the candy and just smeared it all over the eyeball to make it taste sweet, ya know.

So when he got it, well, dat taste all right to Buh Fox.

Buh Fox said, "Pull out de other one!"

When he pulled out de other one, den he called da hounds, said, "Hyeah, hyeah, hyeah!"

And Buh Fox just tore out of there and just butt his fat head on 'gainst the tree.

Buh Rabbit just slick to death![6]

Not only did such stories, with their shrewd and penetrating observations of life, serve as instructional methods for black children, at the same time the appeal that they held for the white master's children as well as for black children helped to continue the black cultural heritage. Such storytelling was allowed by the white master so long as it did not interfere with work, and stories were requested and encouraged on holidays and festive events. It is safe to say that many a secret message passed through these stories at night in the big house or at a harvest festival or at lunchtime in the cotton fields beneath a shade tree at the end of a long row where the white man, shotgun in hand, stood laughing at the stupid blacks telling stories like children.

MUSIC

It was music and songs, however, that constituted the most essential communication among the black slaves. Blacks have a long history of fine expression through rhythm and music. The African civilization of Mali included an elaborate range of string, wind, and percussion instruments, and a long period of professional training was required for its musicians. This musical culture has survived in West Africa for at least a thousand years, and, as suggested in Chapter 6, by its influence upon American music it has enabled the United States to achieve an independence from European musical forms and traditions and to move into new forms. But despite extravagant borrowing from African and Afro-American rhythmic and musical forms, few Americans have ever taken the time or had the interest to understand the nature of these forms. Thus, the survival and deception possibilities of rhythm and intonation were unrecognized by the white masters, although they were inherently known to the black slaves, for whom rhythm could both create and resolve physical tension. The vocalized tone was as important as, and indeed often served the same function as, the verbal double-entendre.

Rhythm and intonation probably constituted the first survival techniques for the black slaves. Here is meant not physical survival but the survival of individualism in an otherwise destroyed personality and the survival of the group through group activity. These techniques first surfaced in the work songs of the slaves. The nature of their work in the cotton fields precluded real freedom of expression; the hands and feet being busy, they could not be used to promote rhythm. That left the slaves' voices, and here intonation became all-important. It was under these conditions that the single call–mass response form developed. Each man developed his own cry, by means of which he could express his own personal sound, his own individualism. In this sense, the work songs were revolutionary, enabling the slaves to join together and at the same time to remain individuals in the face of overt suppression.

Black music has always been the element in black culture most tolerated by whites, and the white slave masters actually encouraged the slaves' work songs, feeling that they helped the slaves work more efficiently. The whites were also fascinated by the slaves' dances and rhythmic songs, and it must have been a great surprise when they learned, probably thanks to some faithful house slave, that the drums which beat for dance and music had also beaten the calls for hundreds of revolts. For all that time they had been oblivious to a code that was more intricate than the Morse code.

The drums had been made from great hollowed-out logs or nail kegs, with skin tightly stretched over one end. Their sound had carried far, and their outlawing constituted a severe blow to the slaves. However, it attests to the great ingenuity of the blacks that they found ways to circumvent the rule against drums. Lydia Parrish wrote: "It always rouses my admiration to see the way in which the McIntosh County 'shouters' tap their heels on the resonant board floor to imitate the beat of the drum their forbears were not allowed to have. Those who hear the records of the musical chants which accompany the ring-shout—made for me by Dr. Lorenzo D. Turner—cannot believe that a drum is not used, though how the effect is achieved with the heels alone—when they barely leave the floor—remains a puzzle."[7] Thus, the slaves retained their drums, in a sense, despite the master's rule.

Other deceptions were more subtle than the drums. The white master rarely apprehended the significance of mood songs, taunt songs, or chants or noticed that certain types of music were played or sung at certain specific times or events. Actually, these songs were more successful deceptive devices than the drums, for they allowed for a large variety of expression. They also were considered by the white masters too emotional to be taken seriously.

The phenomenon of interference that operated in the slaves' learning of standard English also operated in their learning of Western music. They seemed at first unable to master the Western scale because of their own "blue notes," or areas in the scale where tones were smeared together. Simple Western songs, then, as sung by the slaves, were embellished by cries and moans, and the whites reacted by thinking they were both children and born entertainers. Under this guise, the slaves were afforded a considerable amount of secret communication.

RELIGIOUS SERVICES

Clearly the most successful musical or rhythmical media for communication and deception, once they were allowed, were religious songs and chants. For some time after slavery became firmly established in America, white society experienced an intense conflict between its "moral" fervor to "civilize and Christianize the heathen" and its fear for its own physical safety, particularly on plantations where blacks outnumbered whites. Black religious meetings and church services were correctly recognized as vehicles for organization—of resistance, of revolts. But they were more than that; they were outlets for emotionalism, an emotionalism that was rigidly proscribed in nearly every other area of the slaves' lives. What little they had been taught about Christianity was often applicable to their memories of their own African religions. This was true, especially, in the brand of Christianity preached by the Baptists and Methodists with their emphasis upon baptism and the regeneration of the soul.

But even before their formal introduction to Christianity, religion was intensely important to the slaves. Melville J. Herskovits has long been associated with the dispelling of what he has called "the myth of the Negro past," and in his book of the same name he cites the account of a former slave concerning the drive for religious (that is, emotional) expression among the slaves:

On this plantation there were about one hundred and fifty slaves. Of this number, only about ten were Christians. We can easily account for this, for religious services among the slaves were strictly forbidden. But the slaves would steal away into the woods at night and hold services. They would form a circle on their knees around the speaker who would also be on his knees. He would bend forward and speak into or over a vessel of water to drown the sound. If anyone became animated and cried out, the others would quickly stop the noise by placing their hands over the offender's mouth.[8]

When blacks were allowed to conduct religious services, they brought to Christianity their own emphases and their own forms of expression. To be sure, their eager adoption of Christianity contained not a little psychological motivation to absorb the white culture as the powerful and thus "good" culture and to somehow become more "white" through this absorption; the light skin color of those who came to occupy prestigious positions in the church hierarchy attests to this tendency. But of equal importance, at least at first, was the potential for adaptation to their own needs that the church represented. It was a means for social contact, for promoting group coherence, and for expressing overtly emotions that were denied expression in secular life.

This kind of dualism operated and continued to operate in black Christianity. Historically, the black church has functioned both to keep the black man in bondage and to free him from bondage. Only one example of the influence of the black church upon the black psychology is the phenomenon of "aggressive meekness" that older blacks, particularly, assume in the presence of whites. A good example of this phenomenon can be found in Ellison's *Invisible Man,* in the advice an old man on his deathbed gives to his son: "I never told you, but our life is a war and I have been a traitor all my born days, a spy in the enemy's country. . . . Live with your head in the lion's mouth. I want you to overcome 'em with yeses, undermine 'em with grins, agree 'em to death and destruction, let 'em swoller you till they vomit or bust wide open."[9] Aggressive meekness was one of the few means by which blacks could release their hostility, and to this day it continues to be used by blacks in difficult racial situations. While deluding whites, they are, at the same time, acting in the manner that their Christian faith prescribes: "The meek shall inherit the earth," "Suffering will be rewarded," and so on.

This discussion is concerned, however, with black survival techniques, and thus, of the two phenomena that constitute the dualism, or schizophrenia, of the black existence, the positive individualism and life-oriented phenomenon is emphasized. In the time of slavery this positive phenomenon expressed itself in several ways. The favorable atmosphere for simple group coherence—so important at that time when the white masters employed every possible means to discourage it—has already been mentioned. But black Christianity also allowed for many deceptive techniques, not the least of which was the African-influenced, magical, religious chanting. Such chanting was to become a method of "going underground" in order to escape from slavery. The following example, cited in Herskovits's *The Myth of the Negro Past*, illustrates how magic was, almost by its very nature, adapted to "going underground":

Gullah Jack (one of the leaders in Denmark Vesey's insurrection in South Carolina in 1882) was regarded as a sorcerer. . . . He was not only considered invulnerable, but that he could make others so by his charms (consisting chiefly of a crab's claw to be placed in the mouth); and that he could and certainly would provide all his followers with arms.[10]

Jack was probably nothing more than a preacher, but his charm, along with a strange chant that he had remembered from his own African childhood, undoubtedly caused fear and a certain amount of respect among the masters as well as the slaves themselves. Quite probably, Gullah Jack made use of his chanting to help publicize the Vesey revolt as well as others.

SPIRITUALS

Another deceptive technique, developed by black Christianity, was perhaps the most successful of all, and certainly among the most ingenious. This was the use of the southern black spirituals. (The Creoles, who were Catholic, were not successful in employing this medium, for their lyrics were light and gay and often reminiscent of the eighteenth-century French chansons heard in their masters' households.) In fact, southern black spirituals are unequaled both in their emotional expression and in their incorporation of secret messages.

Many spirituals are sung now in white churches. Among them is "Deep River." But few whites who sing "Deep River" realize that it was used by black slaves to announce a meeting at the river:

> Deep River
> My home is over Jordan, Yes
> Deep River, Lord, I want to cross
> over into camp ground.

The slaves on the other side would hear it and wait to hear what time the meeting was going to be held. They would soon hear the song "Let Us Break Bread Together On Our Knees":

> Let us break bread together on our knees,
> Let us break bread together on our knees.

When I fall on my knees with my face to the rising sun,
Oh Lord, have mercy on me.

The time was in the morning and on the west side of the river.

Blacks also used songs to make fun of the master who had told blacks that they were going to a colored heaven and that he, the master, was going to a white heaven. The slaves would then sing this song:

Heaven. Heaven. Heaven, everybody's talking about Heaven.
Oh I got shoes, you got shoes, all God's children got shoes.
When I get to heaven going to put on my shoes and
Walk all around God's heaven,
Heaven, everybody's talking about heaven
Ain't going there ever, ever, heaven,
Going to walk all over God's heaven.

Or they might sing "Did Not Old Pharaoh Get Lost?":

Isaac a ransom, while he lay
Upon an altar bound,
Moses, an infant cast away,
By Pharaoh's daughter found.
Did not old Pharaoh get lost, get lost, get lost,
Did not old Pharaoh get lost in the Red Sea?

When one or a group of slaves was planning an escape and there was danger that the plan would be uncovered, the slaves might sing the shout song, "Get Right, Stay Right." The second and third verses go:

When I meet my neighbor
We talk and have a good time
But I'm always worried
For fear dere's trouble behind!

I may be at church preaching
Or home down on my knee,
Dis worl' is so two-faced
Dere's somebody talking 'bout me.

When slaves were about to begin a revolt, they would be praying and singing that nothing would happen to let the opportunity go by and that they would be able to get out of their oppression. They were disarmed, and they would sing "Sinner Please Don't Let This Harvest Pass":

> Sinner please don't let this harvest pass,
> Repent, repent [but lower and pleading]
> And die and lose your soul at last.

When in fact a slave had just run away and the master, discovering his loss of property, would get his bloodhounds, the other slaves would send the message to the next plantation to let the runaway slave know that the master was on his trail with the bloodhounds. There is only one way to get a bloodhound off your trail, and that is to get into the water. So the message went out and was picked up on one plantation after another until it reached the ears of the runaway slave. The title of that song would be "Wade In The Water":

> Wade in the water, wade in the water.
> Children, God going to trouble the water.

There was one song that the slaves sang to give each other support and to indicate unity in a single goal of freedom, and it was "Walk Together Children":

> Walk together children, don't you get weary.
> Walk together children, don't you get weary. [Repeat]
> There's a great day a coming in this Promised Land.

When the Underground Railroad began, its very existence was a source of hope and support for the slaves and they would remind each other of its existence by singing "The Gospel Train":

> The gospel train is coming,
> I hear it just at hand—
> I hear the car wheels moving,
> And—rumbling thro' the land.
> Get on board—children,
> Get on board.

And finally, there was one song that could mean certain death if the master heard the slaves singing it, but they sang it to their children anyway and passed it on:

> Oh, freedom, oh, oh, freedom
> Oh, freedom—over me
> And before I be a slave I'll be buried in my grave
> And go home to my God and be free.[11]

CONCLUSION

Above all, black psychology is a psychology of survival, and the development of the black language admirably illustrates that psychology. Myriad elements have contributed to and arisen from the blacks' desire to communicate within their subjugated subculture. Even if whites, including educators and linguists, are not aware of the unique dialect and psychology of the black subculture, blacks know it and have known it for a very long time. Even those educated blacks who speak perfect standard English when the situation demands, tend to use the black dialect when speaking with other blacks or when speaking of topics that are identifiably associated with the black culture. Within the confines of the black subculture there are many in-group jokes about the dialect, and it has become a symbol of unity and brotherhood, perhaps the most important basis today of black survival in America.

8
Psychotherapy, Psychoanalysis and the Use of Non-Standard English by African Americans

Over the past two decades there has developed an increased interest in non-standard English as utilized by African Americans. Various terms have been used in describing African Americans' English, including non-standard English, non-standard Negro dialect, and Black English.[1] It is misleading to think in terms of one type of African American dialect, when in fact, many types exist. The factors which help determine the nature of the African American dialect are the region of the country, interaction with other cultures and languages (e.g., Creole), and migratory history. Thus, African American English encompasses a range of dialects including, among others, Southern, Creole, West Indian, and Northern.

Many African Americans are observed with regularity to oscillate between the use of standard English and the use of Black non-standard English. This tendency probably reflects a shifting linguistic comfort based on the situation in which the person finds himself or herself. An African American participating in a predominantly white board of directors meeting would most likely use standard English whereas the same individual would comfortably invoke a Southern non-standard English if participating in a family reunion in rural Mississippi. The term "diglossia" is applicable to this type of shift, and refers to the use by a society of two different languages, dialects or language variants to convey two different values or attitudes. One variety is often learned at home while the other is learned in school.[2] The fact that many African Americans alternate between standard English and some form of Black non-standard English attests to the need of those individuals to exist in two different cultural worlds alternatively or simultaneously.

CREDIBILITY AND THE USE OF LANGUAGE

A number of investigators have attempted to correlate the use of dialects with the attributes and traits which the listener invests in the speaker. R.L. Light in a study in 1977 entitled "Children's Linguistic Attitudes: A Study and Some Implications"[3]

evaluated the perceptions of a group of eight- and nine-year-old children of two African American speakers, one of whom used standard English, the other of whom used Black non-standard English. The terms applied to the Black non-standard speaker were "dumb, ugly, poor, and mean." The speaker who used standard English was described as "smart, pretty, rich, and nice." In an effort to separate ethnicity and standard versus non-standard English use, J.F. Buck[4] contrasted the responses of a group of white college students to Black and white speakers who used standard English. The two standard presentations (Black and white) were rated as most competent while the non-standard were rated as equally competent.

In 1969 the researchers Lambert and Tucker expressed the view that while Black and white college students agree on the superiority of standard English, "Their opions diverge when BNE (Black non-standard English) is contrasted to other non-standard dialect."[5]

According to Feigerson, "Low, or non-standard dialects are viewed as appropriate for use in informal setings and in conversations between in-group members and intimates, while the 'high' (standard) variety is reserved for formal situations and interactions between strangers and the socially dissimilar."[6]

While language is crucial to all human relations and interactions, it is of greater significance in psychotherapy and psychoanalysis. Language is simul-taneously a vehicle for the expression of conflicts, a means of resisting the therapeutic process, and a method of conveying data on a number of historical, emotional, and familial levels.

Before embarking on an exegesis of the role of non-standard English in psychotherapy and psychoanalysis it is relevant to discuss certain works on interracial psychotherapy and psychoanalysis. In the 1950s a series of papers were published, mainly by white psychoanalysts, describing the clinical issues in the treatment of African American patients. In many instances, the titles of the papers underscored the orientations and biases of the authors. Oberndorf[7] was cynical as to the efficacy of interracial therapy because of the divergence of psychological biases. Abraham Kardiner and Lionel Ovesey[8] described the effects of social and economic discrimination upon the personality integration of African Americans. Janet Kennedy[9] focused in her paper on the distrust of African American patients of their white analysts. She regarded the removal of stereotypes held by patients as necessary for the initiation of reconstructive therapy. Viola Bernard[10] felt that in interracial analyses the clinician must expand his personal awareness and control his own conscious and unconscious racial attitudes and reactions. Terry Rodgers[11] described the evolution of an anti-Black white racist during the course of psychoanalysis. Andrew Curry[12] has very adroitly described myths in which Satan, Judas, and Lucifer represent death, darkness, and evil. The transference to the African American therapist utilizes these myths and symbols.

Drs. Judith Schachter and Hugh F. Butts[13] collaborated on a study entitled "Transference and Countertransference in Interracial Analyses." It was the first published psychoanalytic research involving both a white and an African American psychoanalyst reporting on their analysis of contra-racial individuals. The authors conclude the following:

1. Obscuring or overestimating racial stereotypes by analyst or patient may induce a delay in the analysis.

2. Subculturally acceptable pathology may evoke over-reactions, while racial stereotypes may be ignored.

3. Racial differences may catalyze analyses.

This paper underscored the unique features of the transference reactions that are developed by patients in interrracial therapy situations. In addition, language played a significant role in the presentation and resistances of the African American patient, who utilized Black non-standard English at specific times during the progress of therapy. His use of Black non-standard English invariably was a manifestation of resistance.

Dolores O. Morris, Ph.D., in an unpublished paper entitled "The Influence of Ethnicity and Culture on the Analytic Dyad"[14] refers to the significance of language in the psychoanalytic situation. "Language difference is another group of circumstances that has special meaning in the analytic pairing. Bilingual patients bring a complex set of cultural circumstances to the analytic dyad. An understanding of factors of first or second generation levels of assimilation and acculturation are all critical to promoting the analytic process. A careful assessment of the patient's linguistic and sociocultural background, including a preliminary assessment of language dominance and preferences, age when second language was acquired and degree of identification with either the American or culture of heritage should be made."

The studies cited up to this point underscore the transference and countertransference issues extant in those therapies in which therapist and patient differ racially, ethnically or culturally. The studies about to be cited deal specifically with language as a factor in psychotherapy, and more specifically with Black non-standard English and its utilization in psychotherapy.

D.S. Guy in 1979 investigated "Dialect Differences Between Therapist and Patient: Its Influence on the Clinical Evaluations of the Patient."[15] Dr. Guy wished to evaluate the nature of a therapist's evaluation of psychopathology in a patient who used Black non-standard English, as opposed to a patient who used standard English. An actor who on one tape spoke standard English and on another spoke Black non-standard English presented taped material to both black and white therapists. Using variables such as social adjustment, grandiosity, degree of disturbance, and prognosis, the black therapists gave the patient a higher rating when he used Black non-standard English (BNE) than when he used standard English (SE). The white therapists rated the patient higher when SE was used. According to Dr. Guy, her findings indicated a "negative bias on the parts of white therapists and a positive bias on the parts of black therapists."

Knowledge of the terms used by a patient is obviously a necessary prerequisite for the conduct of psychotherapy with that patient. L.C. Schumacher, P.G. Banikotes, and F.G. Banikotes in an effort to investigate the linguistic compatibility of white counselors and Black and white high school students[16] generated a list of the most common words used by each of the three groups and set forth a vocabulary test that was administered to each group. Their findings were that the counselors knew less than one-fifth of the words that the Black students knew and used. The white students scored twice as high as the counselors. Black students knew less than one-third the words that the counselors knew and used. White students scored 10 times better than Black students in terms of their knowledge of the words used by white counselors. The authors interpret their results as indicating that "language differences may significantly inhibit the development of a good therapeutic relationship between white and black students.

In an effort to explain the possible linguistic basis for the disproportionately high reported incidence of schizophrenia among Puerto Ricans in New York City, J.P. Fitzpatrick and R.E. Gould[17] hypothesize that this phenomenon could relate to a lack of understanding on the part of therapists (and evaluators) of Puerto Rican language and culture. It is their view that Puerto Ricans who are struggling to learn English tend to repeat themselves, misconstruct sentences and utilize a vocabulary that is unique to the individual. These investigators feel that these deviations in language may be misinterpreted as indicative of a schizophrenic process. While this study has no direct bearing on the issue of Black non-standard English and psychotherapy, it nonetheless lends itself to interesting speculation. One wonders whether mis-diagnosis of African Americans by white therapists might relate to perceptions of the use of Black dialect as indicating psychopathology.

Marcos[18] in a study parallel to the Fitzpatrick-Gould study found that Spanish-speaking patients were found to have more pathology when evaluated and interviewed in English as contrasted with the level of pathology when interviewed in Spanish. Marcos also commented that individuals who are bilingual evidence constricted affect when conversing in a language other than their native language.

A number of investigators have accorded attention to the language of the therapist as a factor in the course and outcome of psychotherapy. D.M. Russell[19] investigated the relationship between the patient's perceptions of therapist, and therapist's use of Black non-standard English. Black non-standard English was preferred to standard English as a determiner of patient's degree of comfort with a therapist. K.R. Mitchell[20] has suggested that therapists have three types of language at their disposal: public, ordinary, and intimate. Public language is devoid of regional accent and is presented in a slow, regular rhythm. Ordinary speech has a mild regional accent and a casual vocabulary. Intimate speech is characterized by marked regional accent, colorful vocabulary and the use of vulgarities. Mitchell endorses the use of ordinary speech and last-name address as the most suitable for the conduct of psychotherapy. It may be worthwhile at this point to describe in psychodynamic terms that use of language as a vehicle for the expression of emotional conflicts.

We are indebted to Dr. Frantz Fanon and his study "Black Skin, White Masks"[21] for an extremely lucid account of language use in a colonized country. In Martinique, as is true in many colonized nations, the native Martinician identifies with the white oppressor and regards French as the mother tongue, while disparaging Creole, because of it association with blackness. If blackness is denigrated, whiteness is deified, and is equated with purity and goodness. Identifying with the white ego ideal, however, is doomed. Since that ego ideal is unattainable, the subject can only experience frustration, rage and depression. This psychodynamic is operative in any country like the United States that has a ruling, white powerful majority and a subservient unempowered African American minority. The attitudes prevalent in the society will obviously become manifest in an interracial therapy situation involving whites and Blacks.

David M. Russell in an article entitled "Language and Psychotherapy: The Influence of Nonstandard English in Clinical Practise"[22] cites a case vignette underscoring a therapist's failure to understand Black non-standard English, but a rapid non-standard recovery on his part resulted in enhanced communication with the patient.

Client: It be's that way...you know...don't nobody care nothin' 'bout you except if they somethin' in it for them.

Therapist: So you feel that nobody cares about you as a person?

Client: Yeah, I guess you could say it like that.

Therapist: It sounds like I might understand a part of what you meant, but I think there's something there that I'm missing. I'm not sure I understand the whole meaning when you say "it be's that way."

Client: Well, you know—it be's that way...ain't nobody cared about me, not my mom, my family, my wife...sometimes I just feel like it ain't never gonna be no different.

Therapist: So you mean nobody cares, nobody's there that you can count on, not even the least little bit. It be's that way today and it be's that way tomorrow.

Client: Yeah.

The openness on the part of the therapist is not only admirable but extremely therapeutic, and leads to clarification.

Many of the problems cited are not related to malevolence but to ignorance. A knowledge of a patient's language is as vital to an understanding of that patient as is an understanding of his/her psychodynamics.

Milton E. Wilson, in an article entitled "The Significance of Communication in Counseling the Culturally Disadvantaged"[23] emphasizes the importance of understanding the behavioral significance of language differences. "Although they (culturally different clients) may not communicate effectively with professional workers they do communicate effectively among themselves. Middle-class persons who are not highly sensitive to language differences do not receive the culturally disadvantaged effectively because they do not understand the language they speak. Language differences, therefore, are important, for they may affect any realization of desired

behavioral changes through counseling. Left unresolved, language differences can generate mutual rejection."

Wilson goes on to make specific recommendations with respect to the
language that an individual from another culture may utilize. "In the
language area, counselors should permit culturally different clients to use
nonstandard English. Counselors should not criticize the primary language
of their clients. They must not try to obliterate the language being used but
help the clients to see that knowledge of and skills in using standard English
as a second language can make a significant difference in some types of
employment and in some situations related to the satisfaction of needs."

The Dove Counterbalance
Intelligence Test Answers

1.	(d)		16.	(d)
2.	(c)		17.	(b)
3.	(c)		18.	(c)
4.	(c)		19.	(c)
5.	(a)		20.	(c)
6.	(a)		21.	(d)
7.	(c)		22.	(c)
8.	(c)		23.	(a)
9.	(d)		24.	(b)
10.	(c)		25.	(c)
11.	(d)		26.	(c)
12.	(c)		27.	(c)
13.	(c)		28.	(a)
14.	(c)		29.	(c)
15.	(d)		30.	(b)

Notes

CHAPTER 1

1. Theodore Lidz, *The Person* (New York: Basic Books, 1968), p. 169.
2. *Ibid.*
3. Hans G. Furth, *Piaget for Teachers* (Englewood Cliffs, New Jersey: Prentice-Hall, 1970), p. 63.
4. Andrew Billingsley, *Black Families in White America* (Englewood Cliffs, New Jersey: Prentice-Hall, 1968), p. 5.
5. M. M. Lewis, *Thought and Personality in Infancy and Childhood* (New York: Basic Books, 1964), p. 76.
6. J. Piaget, *Dreams and Imitation in Childhood,* trans. C. Gatlengo and F. M. Hodgson (New York: W. W. Norton, 1962), p. 216.
7. Billingsley, *Black Families in White America,* pp. 16–21.
8. *Ibid.*
9. Julius Lester, *Look Out Whitey! black power's gon' get your mama* (New York: Dial Press, 1968), p. 88.
10. Frantz Fanon, *Black Skin, White Masks* (New York: Grove Press, 1967), pp. 17–40.
11. George A. Miller, *New Directions in the Study of Language* (Cambridge, Mass.: M.I.T. Press, 1964), pp. 89–107.
12. *Ibid.,* p. 91.
13. *Ibid.*
14. K. L. Smoke, "An Objective Study of Concept Formation," *Psychol. Monogr.* 42 (1932), No. 191.
15. C. I. Hovlandus and W. Weiss, "Transmission of Information concerning Concepts through Positive and Negative Instances," *J. Exp. Psychol.* 45 (1953), pp. 175–182.
16. P. C. Wason, "The Processing of Positive and Negative Information," *Quart. J. Exp. Psychol.* 11 (1959), pp. 92–107.
17. Joseph Church, *Language and the Discovery of Reality* (New York: Random House, 1963), p. 164.

18. *Ibid.,* p. 166.
19. *Ibid.,* p. 167.
20. Robert I. Hess and Virginia Shipman, "Early Experience and the Socialization of Cognitive Modes in Children," *Black Americans and White Racism (Theory and Research),* ed. Marcil L. Goldschmid (New York: Holt, Rinehart and Winston, 1970), pp. 125–137.
21. George H. Mead, "Language and the Development of the Self," *Readings in Social Psychology* (New York: Henry Holt, 1952), pp. 44–54.
22. *Ibid.,* p. 46.
23. Minutes of the Senate Select Committee on Equal Educational Opportunity, Washington, D.C., July 30, 1971, p. 25.
24. LeRoi Jones, *Dutchman* (New York: William Morrow, 1964), p. 34.
25. Ben Sidran, *Black Talk* (New York: Holt, Rinehart and Winston, 1971), p. 5.
26. *Ibid.*
27. Erik H. Erikson, *Childhood and Society* (New York: W. W. Norton, 1963), p. 290.
28. *Ibid.*

CHAPTER 2

1. Charles A. Pinderhughes, "Understanding Black Power—Processes and Proposals," *American Journal of Psychiatry* 125:11 (1969), pp. 1552–1557.
2. *Ibid.*
3. Abram Kardiner and Lionel Ovesey, *The Mark of Oppression* (Cleveland: World Publishing, 1951), p. 47.
4. Melville Herskovits, *The Myth of the Negro Past* (Boston: Beacon Press, 1958), p. 60.
5. E. Franklin Frazier, *A History of the Negro in the United States* (New York: Macmillan, 1949), p. 87.
6. Kardiner and Ovesey, *The Mark of Oppression,* p. 47.
7. *New York Times,* September 11, 1968, p. 20.
8. Hugh F. Butts, "Skin Color Perception and Self-esteem," *Journal of Negro Education* 32, no. 2 (1963), pp. 122–128.
9. Frantz Fanon, *Black Skin, White Masks* (New York: Grove Press, 1967), p. 12.
10. *Ibid.,* p. 10.
11. *Ibid.,* p. 117.
12. David Caute, *Frantz Fanon* (New York: Viking Press, 1972), p. 5.
13. Herman Melville, *Moby Dick* (New York: Macmillan, 1962), pp. 198–199.
14. Kenneth Clark, "Mental Illness and the Problem of Racial Dis-

crimination," Roche Report, *Frontiers of Clinical Psychiatry* 3, no. 13 (July 1 1966), p. 8.

15. *Ibid.*, p. 8.
16. Erik H. Erikson, *Childhood and Society* (New York: W. W. Norton, 1963), p. 293.
17. Fanon, *Black Skin, White Masks*, p. 117.
18. Adrian Dove, "The Heart of 'Soul,'" *Reader's Digest* (April 1969), pp. 237–242.
19. Hugh F. Butts, "Soul versus Brain or Why Not Pluto Next, Mr. Agnew," *Journal of the National Medical Association* 61, no. 4 (1969), p. 454.

CHAPTER 3

1. Harold G. Lawrence, *African Explorers of the New World*. Monograph reprinted from *The Crisis* (June–July 1962). (New York: Haryou-Act, 1962), p. 2.
2. John G. Jackson, *Introduction to African Civilizations* (New York: University Books, 1970), pp. 234–236.
3. Saunders Redding, *They Came In Chains* (Philadelphia: J. B. Lippincott Co., 1950), pp. 12–13.
4. Quoted in George Philip Krapp, *The English Language in America,* vol. I (New York: Century Co., 1925), pp. 255–265.
5. J. D. Herlein, *Beschryvinge van de volksplantinge Zuriname* (Leeuwarden, 1718), pp. 121–123, retranscribed in William A. Stewart, "Sociolinguistic Factors in the History of American Negro Dialects," *The Florida FL Reporter* (Spring 1967), p. 9.
6. Quoted in Richard Walser, "Negro Dialect in Eighteenth-Century American Drama," *American Speech* 30 (1955), p. 271.
7. Quoted in Guy Carawan and Candie Carawan, *Ain't You Got a Right to the Tree of Life?* (New York: Simon and Schuster, 1968), p. 22.
8. Edward Larocque Tinker, *Gombo: The Creole Dialect of Louisiana* (Worcester, Mass.: The American Antiquarian Society, 1936), p. 8.
9. Lafcadio Hearn, *The American Miscellany,* vol. 2 (New York: Dodd, Mead, 1924), pp. 154–158.
10. Quoted in Stewart, "Sociolinguistic Factors in the History of American Negro Dialects," p. 10.
11. *Ibid.*

CHAPTER 4

1. This discussion is indebted to R. M. R. Hall and Beatrice L. Hall, "The Double-Negative: A Non-Problem," *The Florida FL Reporter* (Spring/Summer 1969), pp. 113–115.

2. J. L. Dillard, "Non-Standard Negro Dialect—Convergence or Divergence?" *The Florida FL Reporter* (1968), p. 7.
3. William A. Stewart, "Continuity and Change in American Negro Dialects." *The Florida FL Reporter* (Spring 1968), p. 24.
4. William A. Stewart, "Sociolinguistic Factors in the History of American Negro Dialects," *The Florida FL Reporter* (Spring 1967), p. 10.
5. Richard Walser, "Negro Dialect in Eighteenth-Century American Drama," *American Speech* 30 (1955), pp. 272–273.
6. Joan C. Baratz and Stephen S. Baratz, "The Social Pathology Model: Historical Basis for Psychology's Denial of the Existence of Negro Culture," paper presented to the American Psychological Association, Washington, D.C., 1969.

CHAPTER 5

1. Dorothy Z. Seymour, "Black English," *Intellectual Digest* 2, no. 6 reprinted from *Commonweal* (February, 1972), p. 78.
2. H. Rap Brown, *Die Nigger Die!* (New York: Dial Press, 1969), p. 26.
3. *Ibid.,* pp. 29–30.
4. Tinker, *Gombo: The Creole Dialect of Louisiana,* p. 18.

CHAPTER 6

1. Cited in Allen Walker Reed, "The Speech of Negroes in Colonial America," *Journal of Negro History* 34 (1939), p. 248.
2. Quoted in Jay B. Hubbell and Douglas Adair, "Robert Munford's 'The Candidates,' " *William and Mary Quarterly* 5 (1948), pp. 217–220.
3. Quoted in Richard Walser, "Negro Dialect in Eighteenth-Century American Drama," *American Speech* 30 (1955), p. 271.
4. *Ibid.,* p. 272.
5. *Ibid.*
6. Tinker, *Gombo: The Creole Dialect of Louisiana,* pp. 12–13.
7. This story was told to one of the authors by an African friend.
8. Ann Sullivan Haskett, "The Representation of Gullah-Influenced Dialect in Twentieth Century South Carolina Prose: 1922–1930." (University of Pennsylvania Ph.D. Dissertation, 1964), pp. 238–241.
9. Quoted in William A. Stewart, "Continuity and Change in American Negro Dialects," *The Florida FL Reporter* (Spring 1968), p. 21, note 12.
10. John Bennett, "Gullah: A Negro Patois," *The South Atlantic Quarterly* 7 (1908), p. 339.
11. *New York Times,* August 25, 1971, p. 35.
12. Clarence Major, *Dictionary of Afro-American Slang* (New York: International Publishers, 1970), pp. 13–14.

13. George Cain, *Blueschild Baby* (New York: McGraw-Hill, 1970), p. 133.
14. Cecil Taylor, *Looking Ahead* (Contemporary Records), liner notes.
15. Langston Hughes, *I Wonder As I Wander* (New York: Hill and Wang, 1956), p. 114.

CHAPTER 7

1. Lydia Parrish, *Slave Songs of the Georgia Sea Islands* (Hatboro, Penn.: Folklore Associates, 1965), p. 20.
2. *Ibid.,* p. 40.
3. *Ibid.,* p. 38.
4. J. Mason Brewer, *American Negro Folklore* (Chicago: Quadrangle Books, 1968), pp. 313–325.
5. *The Negro in Virginia* (New York: Hastings House, 1940), p. 23.
6. Quoted in Brewer, *American Negro Folklore,* pp. 9–10.
7. Parrish, *Slave Songs of the Georgia Sea Islands,* p. 16.
8. Melville J. Herskovits, *The Myth of the Negro Past,* p. 210.
9. Ralph Ellison, *Invisible Man* (New York: Modern Library, 1952), pp. 13–14.
10. Herskovits, *The Myth of the Negro Past,* p. 138. Gullah Jack was born in Africa in a county called M'Choolay Moreema, where a dialect of the Angelo tongue is spoken clear across Africa from sea to sea. This may in some way establish the beginnings of the Gullah dialect. Apparently, Jack's magic was not particularly potent when it came to protecting himself; he was executed in Charleston for his part in the uprising of 1882.
11. Much of this discussion is indebted to Paul K. Winston, prod., "The Dialect of the Black American," (audio presentation). (New York: Western Electric Company, 1971).

CHAPTER 8

1. Dillard, J.L. (1972) *Black English, Its History and Usage in the United States.* New York: Random House.
2. Shaler. D. (1980) *Attitudes Toward English Vernaculars.* Urbana Champaign, Il: University of Illinois, ERIC Document Reproduction Service No. ED 195619.
3. Light, R.L. (1977) *Children's Linguistic Attitudes: A Study and Some Implications.* (ERIC Document Reproduction Service No. ED 154619.
4. Buck, J.F. (1968) "The Effects of Negro and White Dialectal Variations Upon Attitudes of College Students." *Speech Monographs,* 35, 181-86.

5. Lambert, W., & Tucker, G.R. (1969). "White and Negro Listeners' Reactions to Various American-English Dialects," *Social Forces*, 47, 463-468.
6. Ferguson, C.A. (1976) "Diglossia" in P.P. Giglioli (Ed.) *Language and Social Context*. Baltimore: Penguin.
7. Oberndorf, C.P. "Selectivity and Option for Psyschotherapy." *American Journal of Psychiatry*, 110:754-58, 1954.
8. Kardiner, A. and Ovesey, L. *The Mark of Oppression*. Cleveland: World Publishing Co., 1951.
9. Kennedy, Janet A. "Problems Posed in the Analysis of Negro Patients." *Psychiatry*, 15:313-27, 1952.
10. Bernard, Viola W. "Psychoanalysis and Members of Minority Groups." *Journal of the American Psychoanalytic Association*. 1:256-67, 1953
11. Rodgers, Terry. "The Evolution of an Anti-Negro Racist." *The Psychoanalytic Study of Society*. 1:237-47. New York: International Universities Press, 1960.
12. Curry, Andrew. "Transference and the Black Psychotherapist." *Psychoanalytic Review*, 51:7-14, 1964.
13. Schachter, Judith S. and Hugh F. Butts, M.D. "Transference and Countertransference in Interracial Analyses." *Journal of the American Psychoanalytic Association*. Vol. 16, No. 4. October 1968. pp. 792-808.
14. Morris, Dolores O., Ph.D. "The Influence of Ethnicity and Culture on the Analytic Dyad." (Unpublished. February 1, 1992).
15. Guy, D.S. (1979) "Dialect Differences Between Therapist and Patient: Its Influence on the Clinical Evaluations of the Therapist." *Dissertation Abstracts International*, 39, 2985B. (University Microfilms No. 78-22.048).
16. Schumacher, L.C., Banikotes, P.G. and Banikotes, P.G. (1972). "Language Compatibility and Minority Group Counseling." *Journal of Counseling Psychology*, 19, 255-56.
17. Fitzpatrick, J.P. and Gould, R.E. (1976) "Psychotherapy with Bilingual Patients," J. Rubiella (Ed.) *Latin Times*. New York: Freedom Press.
18. Marcos, L.R. (1976) "Bilinguals in Psychotherapy: Language as an Emotional Barrier." *American Journal of Psychotherapy*, 30, 52-56.
19. Russell, D.M. (1983). "The Effect of Therapist Dialect on Clients' Perceptions of the Therapist and Therapy: The Reaction of Black Subjects to Therapists' Use of Black Nonstandard English." *Dissertation*

Abstracts International, 43, 1266 B (University Microfilms No. 82-21700).

20. Mitchell, K.R. (1976) "Clinical Relevance of the Boundary Functions of Language." *Bulletin of the Menninger Clinic*, 40, 641-54.

21. Fanon, Frantz. *Black Skin, White Masks.* Grove Press, New York, 1953.

22. Russell, David M. "Language and Psychotherapy: The Influence on Nontandard English in Clinical Practice.: Clinical Guidelines in Cross-Cultural Mental Health. (Ed.) Lillian Comas-diaz and Ezra E.H. Griffith. New York: John Wiley and Sons, 1985, pp. 33-69.

23. Wilson, Milton E. "The Significance of Communication in Couseling the Culturally Disadvantaged." *The Psychological Consequences of Being a Black American.* (Ed) Roger Wilcox. New York: John Wiley and Co., 1971.

Slang Vocabulary List

anyway If someone is talking to you and you're not interested, you can interrupt by saying "anyway," turning and throwing one palm in the air.

kick me down Means someone "kicked you down" a loan, or a favor.

I ain't stut'n you Contradiction of "I'm not studying" or paying attention to what you are saying or doing.

I'm down with it I understand.

scrubs People who think they're good at something, or are superior for some reason, but are not.

excellent Now more in than "awesome," its syllables are drawn out when spoken. Often paired with "dude."

Jet or dip Leave, used as in "Let's jet."

Work the mix Trying to convince someone to go out with you. Also kick the game, which comes from the opening kickoff of a football game, only in this case, you're ready to start the dating game.

skeezer Someone who scams (trying to find overnight partners) a lot.

em-b Short for embarrassed. "I'm Em-B."

zooted Drunk.

baser Somebody who goofs off in class, skips class a lot or is the class clown.

You're basin' From free-basing cocaine, now means acting silly or off the wall.

Don't catch an attitude Don't get angry. "Attitude" is now nearly always used in a negative sense, like, "he's got a real attitude."

Be mellow The word "mellow" is back from the psychedelic days and now used more often for telling someone to relax than recent words like be cool, chill out, take a chill, pill, or plain ol' chill. Bart simpson's reprise of "Don't have a cow" is passe.

slammed Acknowledge that you or someone else has been insulted.

tired, weak or lame Still popular in same context as "weak effort" or "lame excuse," but often used by itself.

totally I agree. Often paired as "Totally, man."

Glossary of Selected Terms

anywhere Possessing drugs, as "Are you anywhere?"

apple Money.

ass Oneself or a dumb person; "your ass" means the end or destruction of the person referred to.

bad mouth, to To talk about someone maliciously.

ball and chain One's sweetheart or wife.

banjo From African *banjar* (large gourd with a neck of wood attached, and fitted with four strings).

bat Woman.

bear Woman.

big juice Big time racketeer (white), thought to enjoy police protection.

Bird Charlie Yardbird Parker, noted black jazz innovator, generally acknowledged as one of the greatest instrumentalists in American music.

blood Brother; money.

Bogard (Bogart) To act in a forceful manner, like Humphrey Bogart.

bogus False; groundless.

boogie-woogie Fast tempo blues; the type of dancing done to that music.

bread Money.

brother Any black male; usually one having the same point of view as oneself on cultural nationalization.

buckra White man.

bug, to Annoy or irritate.

bull dagger Lesbian.

bulls Police.

burn, to To cook food; to cheat someone.

bustin' suds Washing dishes.

cake Money.

candy man Drug pusher.

chick Woman.

Chuck White man.

cleaner than the Board of Health   Stylishly dressed.

cocktail, to   To stick the last of a marijuana cigarette into the end of a regular cigarette or to wrap it into the torn-off flap of a matchbook because it is too short to hold in the hand.

cooter   From African *kuta,* a kind of turtle.

crazy   A term of endearment; having a special way of looking at a particular situation.

creep   A cheat or two-time.

Creole   From *Creo,* from Sierra Leone African *Krio,* language of domestic life—courtship or marriage, death, joy, deepest grief.

crumbcrushers   Small children.

deal   Woman.

devil   White man.

did a nickel [at Attica]   Served five months.

dig, to   From African *degan,* to understand; a call for attention.

dozens   A word game in which close members of the family are degraded.

down home   Southern.

dust   Money.

fish   Woman.

five calenders   Five months.

flew coy   Became coquettish.

flipping out   Having a temporary psychotic reaction to drugs.

fox   Woman.

freebees   Things or ideas that do not cost money.

fucked up   High on dope.

fulafafa   Woodpecker.

Georgia ham   Watermelon.

gofer   One who "goes for" something; expression of approval.

grape   Money.

gray   White person.

gray boy   White man.

groovy   Excellent, enjoyable.

guy   Man.

hammer   Woman.

hangout   A meeting place for a gang.

hang-up   Preoccupation.

happy shop   Liquor store.

hawk   Cold wind.

hawk, to   To walk rapidly.

hep   Understand.

hincty   Snobbish, uppity.

hip   Understand.

home boy   Person from the South, same town or state as yourself.

honkie or **honky** White man.

hustle To survive by any means possible.

hustlers don't call showdowns Beggars can't be choosers.

ice, to To ignore.

iced Ignored; imprisoned and in solitary confinement.

jack Money.

jam, to To make exciting music; to party.

jazz A type or style of music, noise, static; cluttered conversation used to confuse.

jig From African *juge,* fast dance.

Jim Term of address to a male.

jitter Dance.

jitter bug A dance done to swing music.

jitter doll A woman who loves dancing.

jive Dope.

jones Hard dope.

know about it Dig; understand.

laid in the aisle Well dressed, stylish.

lam, to To run; to flee.

leg Woman.

let it all hang out To be uninhibited, free.

letter from home Watermelon.

like A word that bridges gaps in spoken sentences.

main squeeze A man's favorite woman.

mag Magazine.

man, the Whites in power; the police.

masser planter Any superior.

mickey mouse White man.

mink A woman.

Mr. Charley White man.

nod Hair; stupor-like state experienced by a junkie succumbing to drugs.

ofay White man.

O.K. Correct; right; warranting approval.

out to lunch Being in a state in which one does not or cannot understand, either because he is ignoring another person or because their points of view conflict.

paddy White man.

peckerwood Southern white.

pimp talk Origin Chicago; affixing of a nonsense syllable to certain syllables of words.

pounds Money.

pull your coattail Make you aware.

raincoats Prophylactics.

raise, to Get out of jail.

rap, to   To tell the truth, uncluttered and to the point; to talk.

right on   Tell the truth; say what must be said.

rip off, to   To steal.

run it down   Keep talking; hurry up and tell me.

scag   Heroin.

shit ass   One who talks nonsense.

short   Automobile.

shot through the grease   Given a hard time.

shout   The Arabic *saut,* to run and walk around.

side   Woman.

signify, to   To berate, degrade.

sister   Any black female, usually one having the same point of view as oneself on cultural nationalization.

smoke   Drugs.

snag   Unattractive woman.

soft leg   Woman.

soul   The sensitivity inherent in the blues; the black heritage; feeling for one's roots; the humanism of blacks.

squeeze   Girl friend; boyfriend; intimate acquaintance.

stallion   Tall, attractive woman.

strung out   Addicted, especially to a heavy drug.

stumpers   Shoes.

sweat box   Crowded party.

tabby houses   From African *tabax,* slave quarters built out of oyster shells, sand.

tackies   From West African *taki* (horse), small wild horse in the marshes of the Sea Islands of South Carolina and Georgia.

that's your weight   That's your responsibility.

toggle board   From West African *dzogal* (to rise), see-saw.

tote   From Congo *tota* (to pick up), to carry something.

trap   The military draft board.

trogans   Prophylactics.

uh-huh and uh uh   Yes and no.

wail   A beautiful delivery, especially in the performance of music.

walisapapa   Woodpecker.

whale, to   Run fast.

wild   Deeply satisfying.

wine   Money.

Selected Bibliography

Baratz, Joan C., and Stephen S. Baratz. "The Social Pathology Model: Historical Basis for Psychology's Denial of the Existence of Negro Culture." Washington, D.C.: American Psychological Association paper, 1969.

Bennett, John. "Gullah: A Negro Patois," *The South Atlantic Quarterly* 7 (October 1908): 335–349.

Billingsley, Andrew. *Black Families in White America*. Englewood Cliffs, New Jersey: Prentice-Hall, Inc., 1968.

Brewer, J. Mason. *American Negro Folklore*. Chicago: Quadrangle Books, 1968.

Brown, H. Rap. *Die Nigger Die!* New York: Dial Press, 1969.

Cain, George. *Blueschild Baby*. New York: McGraw-Hill, 1970.

Carawan, Guy, and Candie Carawan, eds. *Ain't You Got a Right to the Tree of Life? The People of Johns Island, South Carolina—Their Faces, Their Words and Their Songs*. New York: Simon and Schuster, 1968.

Dillard, J. L. "Non-Standard Negro Dialects—Convergence or Divergence?," *The Florida FL Reporetr* (Fall 1968), 6–8.

Ellison, Ralph. *Invisible Man*. New York: Modern Library, 1952.

Furth, Hans G. *Piaget for Teachers*. Englewood Cliffs, New Jersey: Prentice-Hall, Inc., 1970.

Hall, R. M. R., and Beatrice Hall. "The Double-Negative: A Non-Problem," *The Florida FL Reporter* (Spring/Summer 1969), 113–115.

Haskell, Ann Sullivan. "The Representation of Gullah-Influenced Dialect in Twentieth Century South Carolina Prose: 1922–1930." University of Pennsylvania Ph.D. dissertation, 1964.

Hearn, Lafcadio. *The American Miscellany*. 2 vols. New York: Dodd, Mead, 1924.

Herskovits, Melville J. *The Myth of the Negro Past*. Boston: Beacon Press, 1958.

"How to Talk Black," *Newsweek* (February 21, 1972), 79.

98   Selected Bibliography

Hubbell, Jay B. and Douglas Adair. "Robert Munford's 'The Candidates,'" *William and Mary Quarterly* 5 (1948), 217–220.

Hughes, Langston. *I Wonder As I Wander.* New York: Hill and Wang, 1956.

Jackson, John G. *Introduction to African Civilizations.* New York: University Books, 1970.

Johnson, Kenneth B. "Teachers' Attitude toward the Nonstandard Negro Dialect—Let's Change it, or, False Assumptions Teachers Make About the Nonstandard Negro Dialect." Unpublished paper, University of Illinois at Chicago Circle, 1971.

———. "The Language of Black Children: Instructional Implications," *Racial Crisis in American Education,* ed. Robert L. Green. Chicago: Follett, 1970.

Krapp, George Philip. *The English Language in America,* vol. 1. New York: Century, 1925.

Lawrence, Harold G. *African Explorers of the New World.* New York: Haryou-Act, 1962.

Locke, Alain. *Negro Art: Past and Present (The Negro and His Music,* ed. William Loren Katz). New York: Arno Press and the *New York Times,* 1969.

Major, Clarence. *Dictionary of Afro-American Slang.* New York: International Publishers, 1970.

Mitchell, Henry H. *Black Preaching.* Philadelphia: J. B. Lippincott, 1970.

New York Times, August 25, 1971, 35.

New York Times, November 22, 1971, 36.

Parrish, Lydia. *Slave Songs of the Georgia Sea Islands.* Hatboro, Penn.: Folklore Associates, 1965.

Pei, Mario. *All about Language.* Philadelphia: J. B. Lippincott, 1954.

Piaget, J. *Dreams and Imitation in Childhood,* translated by C. Gatlengo and F. M. Hodgson. New York: W. W. Norton, 1962.

Postman, Neil, Charles Weingartner, and Terence P. Morgan, eds. *Language in America.* New York: Dell, 1969.

Postman, Neil, and Charles Weingartner. *Linguistics: A Revolution in Teaching.* New York: Dell, 1966.

Redding, Saunders. *They Came in Chains.* Philadelphia: J. B. Lippincott, Philadelphia, 1950.

Reed, Allen Walker. "The Speech of Negroes in Colonial America," *Journal of Negro History,* 24 (1939), 245–260.

Seymour, Dorothy Z. "Black English," reprinted from *Commonweal, Intellectual Digest* 2, no. 6 (February 1972), 78–80.

Sidran, Ben. *Black Talk.* New York: Holt, Rinehart & Winston, 1971.

Sierra Leone Language Review (African Language Review), ed. David Dalby, 1964–1966. Sierra Leone: Fourah Bay College, University of Sierra Leone.

Skinner, Tom. *How Black is the Gospel?* Philadelphia: J. B. Lippincott, 1970.

Spellman, A. B. *Black Music: Four Lives.* New York: Schocken Books, 1970.

Stewart, William A. "Continuity and Change in American Negro Dialects," *The Florida FL Reporter* (Spring 1968), 20–25.

———. "Sociolinguistic Factors in the History of American Negro Dialects," *The Florida FL Reporter* (Spring 1967), 7–10.

Taylor, Cecil B. *Looking Ahead.* Contemporary Records.

The Negro in Virginia. New York: Hastings House, 1940.

Tinker, Edward Larocque. *Gombo Comes to Philadelphia.* Worcester, Mass.: The American Antiquarian Society, 1957.

———. *Gombo: The Creole Dialect of Louisiana.* Worcester, Mass.: The American Antiquarian Society, 1936.

Turner, Lorenzo D. *Africanisms in the Gullah Dialect.* New York: Arno Press, 1969.

Walser, Richard. "Negro Dialect in Eighteenth-Century American Drama," *American Speech* 30 (1955), 269–276.

Winston, Paul K., prod. "The Dialect of the Black American," audio presentation. New York: Western Electric Co., 1971.

Index

under slavery, 18
Movies. *See* Mass media
Munford, Robert, 55
Music
  African heritage in, 67-69
  and language development, 13
  as survival mechanism, 67-69
  blacks influence on, 60-62
  blues, 61, 69
  instruments, 67-68
  jazz, 59-60, 61-62
  popular music, 60
  spirituals, 60, 71-73
  universality of, 29

Nigger-pidgin, 6
Nonverbal children. *See* Speech development
Nuclear family, 5-6
Nurturing. *See* Mothering

Oberndorf, 76-77
Oppression. *See* Racism
Ovesey, Lionel, 16, 18, 77

Paranoia, 15-16
Parrish, Lydia, 63-64, 68
Piaget, J., 3, 4-5
Pidgin English
  in Africa, 30-31, 32, 43
  in America, 30-35, 36
  in literature, 31, 32
  in West Indies, 31-32
  "nigger pidgin," 6. *See also* Dialects
Pinderhughes, Charles A., 15
Police, 18
Pragmatics, 6-7
Preschool child, 10
Productivity, in language, 7
Pronunciation, of black English, 42-44
Proverbs
  as survival mechanisms, 64-66
  examples of, 65
Psycholinguistics, 6-7
Psychology
  and linguistics, 6-7
  of racism, 15-27
Public language, 79

Quinn, Arthur Hobson, 55

Racial inferiority, theory of
  and black language, 34-35, 40, 44, 49, 50
  and teacher attitudes, 52-53
Racism
  adaptation to, 3, 5-6, 10-11, 12, 14, 15, 16-17, 18, 25-27
  and colonialism, 6, 23-24
  and language. *See* Black English; Dialects, Pidgin English
  and sexuality, 161
  and stereo types, 18-19
  effects on whites of, 16, 24-25
  Frantz Fanon on, 23
  origins of, 15-16
  psychology of, 15-27
  soul as response to, 2@27 Reading ability, 50
Redding, Saunders, 30-31
Reich, Wilhelm, 54
Religion
  and skin color, 70
  under slavery, 69-73
  universality of, 29
Rock culture, 62
Rogers, Terry, 77
Russell, D.M., 79, 80

Schachter, Judith, 77
Schools
  and black English, 44, 45-46, 49-53, 74
  out-of-school behavior, 50-52
  reading ability in, 50
  teacher attitudes in, 46, 52-53
  verbal behavior in, 49-50
Schizophrenia, 78-79
Schumaker, L.C., 78
Self-development, 9
Self-esteem
  and black English, 46
  and skin color, 19-23
  California Test of Personality (C.T.P.) for, 19, Table 1, 20-22, Table 4, 23